City of Kaus
REUNION

BOOK 4

DANI HOOTS

Reunion
City of Kaus, #4
First Edition © 2023 FoxTales Press
Edits by Victory Editing
Cover Art Copyright © 2021 Mona Finden
Cover Format Copyright © 2023 by Biserka
Designs

ISBN for Paperback: 978-1-956495-12-6
ISBN for Hardcover: 978-1-956495-13-3

"Pride is not the opposite of shame, but it's source. True humility is the only antidote to shame."

—Uncle Iroh

CHAPTER I

Zach

Snow gently sprinkled from the sky and caught on every surface, including my clothes, my red hair, and my matching beard. The longer I stood outside, the whiter my beard always seemed to become, even if it wasn't that long. The snowy landscape seemed to go on for miles. I let out a sigh as I pulled my coat closed and listened to the creaking of the evergreens around me. I had a feeling even they didn't want to be here, but it wasn't as if a tree could get up and move—or at least not in real life. I had read some books where trees were like people and could make their way across the land. Since reading that book, I kept my eye on trees, but so far I hadn't witnessed anything like that happening.

A squirrel jumped out of the snow and up a tree, screaming at me as it probably went up to take some food to its hiding place. I couldn't believe any sort of creature could make its life out here, but apparently it could, as we had found a few creatures we could hunt for food to get us through the winter. Not only that, but we also found some berries and greenery we could harvest and eat for the time being. I wasn't sure how we were going to stock up for the winter, however.

Living in this sort of terrain was not ideal even if we could change into Lyrans if we wanted to. But we hadn't changed our appearance. And there were many reasons for that. Many that had to do with the psychological trauma we had faced when we were younger. That, and because Gabe couldn't transform, and we didn't want him to freeze while we were fine. It wasn't too cold yet, at least. Perhaps our views would change once winter came.

I went back into the makeshift tent building Cor and I had created for shelter thus far. Cor was sitting next to Gabe, watching him sleep. Ellie was in the other bed, still healing from her gunshot wound and, after much resistance, was staying still and resting. She kept trying to help us set up the camp, and Cor and I kept forcing her to lie back down. After we promised she could do all the galivanting she wanted after she healed, she gave in. I had a feeling the real reason she stopped, however, was because the wound was aching mighty fierce, and she just didn't want to admit it.

Luckily, as we'd headed into the treacherous landscape, we came upon an abandoned home, or I should say shed. We knew it would be too dangerous to stop there since it was close to the snow line and Gabe's father was looking for us. We were able to find some resources, however, which we took and have been using, including blankets, rudimentary medical supplies, and whiskey. Ellie was hogging the whiskey and using it to heal herself, or so she claimed, and we used some of the medicine on Gabe to help him heal from the poisoning.

I sat down next to Ellie as she snored, and I glanced over at the bed that Gabe was on. I couldn't believe all that had happened to him in the past two weeks. He was one of the nicest, most genuine persons I knew, and yet had to deal with all this shit. He didn't deserve it—none of us deserved it. None of the Kausians deserved what Jonathan and Byron had done to them.

Cor gently caressed Gabe's face as he frowned. I could only imagine what was going through his mind. When both Ellie and Gabe were injured and needed help getting out of Jonathan's manor, the dilemma on his face was something I would never forget. He cared for them both, and he didn't know who to choose to save at that moment. I was glad I was there to help, but if I hadn't been, I wondered whom he would have saved. Perhaps he would have chosen Ellie simply because she weighed less and was easier for him to move, not to mention she was still conscious and could at least help a little.

But if he didn't have to consider that—if he had to save one life or another—what would have been his choice?

Although I wanted to know the answer, I knew it wouldn't have been fair to ask. I wouldn't have been able to pick between two people I cared about most. I would have done anything I could to save them both or died trying. Question was—would he have risked his own skin for either of them?

Ellie began to stir. Both Cor and I turned our attention to her. Her eyes flickered open as she snorted, which made me smile. Same ol' Ellie, even after everything that had happened.

"Where in the goddess are we?" she moaned as she stretched. She grimaced as she moved the arm that was wounded.

I watched as realization struck and all the memories of the past few days came back.

"How's Gabe?" she asked as she turned to him.

Cor answered as he caressed Gabe's cheek. "He's still sleeping, but he looks a lot better. We gave him that medicine we found in that old home."

She nodded slowly. "That's right. Everything has

been a blur."

I rolled my eyes. "That's because you had a gunshot and have been treating yourself with moonshine."

Ellie shot me a look. "You told me I had to stay in bed. What else was I going to do?"

I stretched as I stood up. "That's fair. Now let me help you change the bandage."

"If I have learned anything in the past couple of days"—Cor sighed as he turned to the two of us—"it's that you aren't that good at changing bandages."

I frowned, even though I knew he was right. "We've been getting by fine before you came along, you know."

"And it was a miracle you two didn't die from an infection. Let me change it."

I gestured to Ellie. "Be my guest. But just a warning, she bites."

Cor cocked a grin. "Don't I know it."

Ellie rolled her eyes, but I noticed her blush a little.

I pretended to gag as Cor grabbed some clean

cloth. There were only a few more spare cloths, so either we would have to find some disinfectant or maybe Ellie would be good enough to not need dressing any longer. Hopefully it was the latter.

Removing the previous gauze, Cor examined the wound. "Looks to be healing well. I think you should be able to move around fine tomorrow."

Ellie smiled. "Well, that's a relief. I'm really bored."

Both Cor and I laughed. We knew Ellie couldn't sit still. She never could even when we were kids. She always wanted to be on the next adventure, whether it be fishing for the biggest catfish in the lake or sneaking into the amusement park on the moon.

The memories felt as if they were a stab to the heart. I missed those days. They were simpler, and while we still had to worry about being killed even back then, at least things weren't as horrible as they were now. Or perhaps they were, and we never realized to what extent others wanted us dead.

As Cor changed her dressing, Ellie's eyes drifted over to Gabe. Even in the short amount of time that we had all been together, we had grown close to Gabe. He was kind and caring—not someone who should have to worry about being poisoned by his own father.

"He'll be fine," Cor commented, also noticing that Ellie was watching Gabe. "He's a fighter."

"That he definitely is. Never would I have imagined he would be able to take all this. He seemed so… soft when I met him. An easy mark."

Cor chuckled. "Yeah, he gives off that vibe. Although I have saved him many times, he's also saved me quite a few. Even if it meant risking his own life."

We had witnessed that when he put his life on the line to get into Byron's home to save Cor. I never thought it would end with Gabe's father killing Byron, showing his true colors, and poisoning his own son.

"We're lucky we found that shack at the snowline. Wish we could thank whoever left those supplies," Ellie added.

"It's likely he's dead. No one in their right mind would have left all that willingly," Cor said under his breath.

All of us were silent. We knew the odds were against the person or people who were living there. This terrain was harsh, and although they tried to stay close to the edge of the mountain, it was likely they could have been attacked by bandits. Though if that were the case, then the supplies wouldn't have been there. They must have left or died recently even if some of the windows had been broken and there was a layer of dust on everything.

"We aren't going to survive out here, are we?" Ellie more stated than asked.

Cor and I glanced at each other. The same thought had crossed our minds countless times.

Cor responded, "The odds are slim, yes, but they are slimmer if we stayed in the towns. Byron was always one step ahead of us, but Jonathan is even more devious and probably has our photos in every bar and pub in every town in all the zones. With the four of us, we can harvest enough supplies for the winter, then later, after it all blows over and everyone is dead, we can raid a town and get some supplies."

I frowned. "Cor, that's not funny."

"He's right though." Ellie sighed. "Jonathan is going to destroy this entire planet, and we're letting him do it."

We were all silent for a moment. There was still a sting of guilt in all our hearts, but we couldn't have stayed there. If we had, we would have died. It wasn't as if anyone stood up for our kind—it wasn't as if they had tried to help us when our home was destroyed. No, they all believed it was needed and that we needed to be destroyed. They bought it all and let genocide happen.

And yet…

Cor spoke before I could let my heart feel guilt. "They deserted us in our time of need. We're only four people, and there are a lot of them. They can handle it."

Ellie turned her attention to Cor. "It took the actions of one person to destroy a zone, and I believe it can take the actions of one person to save another one."

I had to hold back the whistle I wanted to make. That was a low blow even if it was true. Cor didn't say a word as he finished bandaging Ellie. He stood up and left our little hut. I watched as the piece of wood shut behind him, letting in cold air for a brief moment. It was still the warmer months, meaning this winter was going to be a lot colder.

"That was rather harsh," I commented as I moved back next to Ellie.

"Yeah, well, I'm in a foul mood."

"Still, just because you feel like shit, you shouldn't take out your frustrations on someone else. We're all tired and cold and feel helpless. Don't forget that." She frowned, and I grabbed her hand and squeezed it. "You'll heal fine and can help with the hunting and the gathering of resources for the winter. Gabe as well. We're going to be with each other for a long time. I wouldn't recommend burning bridges yet."

Ellie let out a sigh. "I'll apologize to Cor when he gets back. But he already knows all the things I said were true, and he needs to face them."

"We all have things we need to face. Even if we don't want to."

CHAPTER II

Cor

I regretted leaving the makeshift hut we had the moment I stepped outside. It was cold, and I should have grabbed another layer, not that it would have helped much. I would just have to suffer, which was fine. I wasn't going to be gone long—I just needed to walk this one off.

Because Ellie was right—it did take one person to destroy our nation. And it was me. It was my fault. I had to live with that fact.

It would be a weight on my shoulders I would have to carry for the rest of my life. That much I knew. It was a heavy burden but not one I wanted anyone else to carry. That's why I had wished Ellie, Gabe, and Zach would have left me to deal with Byron. This wasn't their fight. It was mine.

Well, come to find out that wasn't completely true. Byron had been Gabe's uncle, and there was a lot going on there. It was strange how small the world could be and how our fates were so intertwined. Perhaps we were destined to take them down. Or perhaps we had simply lucked out this entire time.

Not wanting to go back in there and tell Ellie she was right, or at least not yet, I decided to take a brief walk around the area and make sure there weren't any dangers surrounding us other than cold, crisp air. Zach and I had taken turns to check out the area and to inventory what we could harvest and hunt for food before the winter came. So far we had found a couple of things that we could live off of, but that would change in the coming months.

I did not look forward to winter. It was going to be miserable, and I wasn't even sure we would survive to spring. From the stories I heard, it was nearly impossible to live out here, but then again, many said the area Kaus laid was inhabitable. If you learned how to react to weather and surroundings instead of fighting them, life was much easier. All of us Kausians knew that to be a fact.

We had to learn to adapt, or we would all be dead. That was the Kausian motto.

Rubbing my temple, I tried to remember all the training we were given as children about living in the mountains. We were trained in case we had to leave. If the nation had known about the attack before it happened, they probably would have all moved out here. If only there had been a way to warn everyone.

I ventured toward the other side of the rocky hill we had built against. There was a whole lot more snow and ice, just as I expected. Everything was silent other than the trees creaking as they swayed back and forth. The snow crunched under my boots. I didn't like how silent it was—give me a roaring city any day. The silence like this made it easy for my thoughts to take over. The bars and saloons we found ourselves in most nights than not kept the voices in my head silent—the voices that liked to remind me of what I had done.

Trying to shake it all off, I decided I should gather some firewood for the makeshift stove fireplace we made. I peered around for sticks and twigs. We would have to make an axe somehow later. I wasn't sure how we would manage that, though, as I wasn't the handiest in the wilderness. We were taught some survival skills when we were younger, but after the destruction of Kaus, I had learned quickly that money could buy a lot more than I could make out in nature, so I focused on those skills rather than how to make tools and whatnot. I knew Ellie had some knives, so it was possible to use that to get some wood. Perhaps we could make a stone axe, and by we, I meant Ellie or Zach.

I grabbed some balsam fir needles to help with the fire, along with some resin. These trees would be very helpful in the winter since balsam fir resin was highly flammable. It helped start and keep the fire going. At least I knew what plants to use out in the wilderness—that much had stuck.

After I gathered a handful of supplies, I bit my lip. I still didn't want to go back to the camp. Ellie was there, and I didn't want to admit I was being childish, but my hands were already getting full of sticks. I decided I would take them to the campsite, set them outside, and then venture off toward the lake.

Giving into the temptation of not wanting to see Ellie yet, I headed toward where the rest of the group was to set all of this down and then leave again. Or perhaps I could peer inside to see if Ellie had fallen back asleep—then I could get out of this snow, and I wouldn't have to face her quite yet. Odds were she was still awake and was awaiting my return. And was probably sipping on that moonshine we had found, and she had claimed it was the answer to her bullet wound. Once that ran out, however, I wondered how she was going to get by. Unless she wanted to make her own brew, she was going to be going a long while without liquor. I was not looking forward to when she faced that realization.

It was strange to think such things like this of Ellie. Just a few weeks ago I had been on the run from her—knowing she was always on my heels trying to find me. Now I worried about whether or not she was getting enough to eat and was healing fine. How could so much change in such a short amount of time?

Perhaps it was because I still loved her, and my heart would never stop caring for her—even if I did have someone else… even if we both should move on… even if she deserved much better than me.

Thoughts of Gabe entered my mind, and I began to wonder what was going to happen when he woke again. We were able to keep him warm enough, sure, but I wasn't sure how he was going to handle the winter snow. Sirians lived underwater, so I would assume it would be fine, but they also didn't have much of a temperature change in the water— at least not where the city was since it was so deep.

He had been close to dying, and I still wasn't

sure how I felt about it all. Sure, he had almost died a few times, but this was different. This time it was someone he trusted—someone who should have been trying to keep him safe. His own father had tried to kill him.

He was only alive because he was half-human, which was the only instance that came in handy for him. We had all eaten that food—did Jonathan know that it wasn't poisonous to Kausians, or did that matter to him? The odds were he didn't care since he was going to kill us anyway. But poison? It was such a cowardly way to kill someone. And it was not a way I wanted to die.

As I made it back to the camp, I found Zach outside, staring up at the sky. I glanced up but found nothing but clouds and the two suns shining. I always found it strange how the suns could be out, and it still felt cold. Didn't seem right, even if Byron had taught me it was because we were farther away from both of them.

I didn't like that I had learned so much from Byron. He had taken time to educate me so that I could apply to a university. He led me to believe he would sponsor me. But it all had been a ruse to get on my good side so I would tell him the secrets of Kaus. I felt more of a fool each and every time I thought about it, which was more often than not. But at least I had gained a lot of knowledge out of it—knowledge that would come in handy more often than not, but it wasn't worth the price of my home. Nothing was.

I stepped up to Zach, and he turned his attention to me. He nodded to the sticks in my arms. "Way to be productive."

I shrugged. "I felt stupid walking off like that and needed something to do."

"Usually when I have to cool my temper off, I just walk around in circles."

"There was a lot of that too."

He was quiet for a moment. I heard a chunk of snow fall off a branch not too far from us. He sighed. "Ellie is sorry for what she said. She didn't mean—"

I shook my head. "No, I deserved it. I didn't run off like that because I was mad at her—I ran off like that because she was right. But I need to stop living in the past and plan for the future. We all do.”

“Yeah, I suppose we do. But the future is so unstable it's kind of hard.”

I set the bundle of sticks down. “You can say that again. But we can just keep on living. Or at least try to. I'm not sure if we'll be able to help the world with only the four of us, but I know together we might be able to keep each other safe. I mean, after all we've been through, this place should be a piece of cake.”

“I hope so, but I don't know if we can be too sure.”

“We can always venture down the mountain if we need to.”

“But then there might be bandits.” Zach sighed. “I hate bandits. They are merciless. And they don't give up.”

“Depending on how many there are, we could probably take them.”

Zach shook his head. “No, I'm done with killing. Even if they are horrible people who wouldn't think twice about killing me, I don't want to be the one who ends their life. Enough is enough for me. I don't think I can take much more of it."

I understood what he was saying. I didn't want to see any more blood either. But that was the way of this life, and my hands were already soaked in red. I turned toward where the frozen lake was. "I'm going to go check out the lake again. Can you keep an eye on things?"

Zach nodded. "Sure. I can do that."

Turning, I headed toward the lake that was only about a quarter of a mile away. I took note of more plants we could harvest when the time was right. Perhaps we could survive out here. Unlike most people, we knew our plants and territory well. Kausians were trained to survive.

I made it to the lake and stared. It was large—almost as big as a small town. The odds were there were fish in there, but it was all frozen over. I wasn't sure how thin the ice was and didn't want to find out the hard way by myself. We would have to investigate and then figure out a way to make a hole in the ice so we could fish. We would also need some string to make a fishing rod.

I sighed as I sat down in the snow. There was so much to do still. Even if winter was months away, I worried we wouldn't be ready. I wished we had enough time to have gone to some stores before escaping to this place. We were lucky to find that old shed. Otherwise, there would have been a lot more issues we would have had to face.

Staring up at the sky, I took a deep breath. We would survive. We had to.

CHAPTER III

Ellie

I fell asleep before Cor came back. It was as if that was the only thing I could do these days. I knew I needed to heal, but I hated simply sitting around like this. Though if I could get up, what was I going to do? Just wander the wilderness until the world ends? It was just the four of us out here. There was no one else we would interact with. No one to have conversations with. No one to get to know and become friends with. But on the other hand, it meant there would be no one to try to kill us. We wouldn't have to be constantly looking over our shoulders.

Was that true, though? Would Jonathan not keep searching for us out here? Would he give up just because we were in the mountains? Would he assume we would die during the first winter out here, or retreat back into the towns where he could capture us? So many questions filled my mind, and I began to wonder if I could really stay out here where there were no other people. While I knew most people hated my kind and looked at me with such great animosity, it was better than nothing. Or, perhaps, with each person I met, I thought perhaps some would accept us.

There was that feeling in my chest again. What was it? Remorse? Sadness? Fear? All the above? I missed my family. I missed my friends even if it was just Cor and Zach I was closest to growing up. Back then, at least there was some sort of community. At least there were people we could talk to who understood our hardships.

But all that was gone. Now we were alone—truly alone—in the mountains for who knew how long.

Rising up, I decided it would be best if I stood and moved around for a bit. My legs were getting restless, and my mind always spiraled if I stayed still. Just as it always had, especially after our home was destroyed. The what ifs always filled my mind in the darkest of nights.

"Whoa, where do you think you're going?" Cor asked as he moved toward me from Gabe's bed.

I shrugged him off. "I need to move around. Get the blood flowing and all."

"I don't know if that is wise…"

"You said it yourself that I was healing nicely. Also, I want to see the beautiful mountain scenery. Although it's going to be a cold, miserable time, the mountains aren't something we get to see often. But I guess we will have a lot of time to see it all, won't we?"

"Just… let me help you."

I glanced around as he helped me up. "Where's Zach?"

"Wandering around somewhere."

"Will Gabe be all right on his own?"

Cor nodded. "Yeah, he's still just asleep. And we won't be long. Zach should be back soon anyway."

He grabbed my good arm and helped me to the makeshift door. He opened it up, and the cold, frosty air hit me like a wall.

"Oh, that's freezing," I commented. "And here I thought it was already cold in our new little home."

"We're going to have to work on insulating the place before winter comes, but I think we'll be able to manage. I can show you how we built the place so we can add moss and all that to keep it warm inside. Or, at least, I hope it will keep it warm outside."

Cor helped me outside, and sure enough, he and Zach had taken pieces of the shack we had found earlier and surrounded the side of a cliff. There were plenty of holes we would need to fill, but it would make do. For now, at least. We may decide otherwise when the first blizzard comes.

"Looks nice. Can't wait to see it all covered in ten or so feet of snow."

"Yeah, we're going to have to reinforce it to

make sure the roof doesn't collapse. Zach said the two of you have built a home before."

I nodded slowly as the memories of watching it burn down came back. "Yeah, we did."

"Why didn't you stay?"

I gave him a look.

He nodded. "Ah, right. Bandits."

"Yup. A group of them came and burned it down. That's when we decided we should always be on the move. And, you know, wanting revenge on you kept us on the move as well. You never seemed to stay still."

I glanced at him to find his eyes glazed over. They did that any time he went to a different place in his mind. I took a deep breath and squeezed his hand.

"Hey, I wanted to tell you sorry. For earlier. I shouldn't have said that. I was just irritated with our circumstances, and I took it out on you."

He shook his head. "You don't have anything to be sorry about. It was true. It was because of me that all this happened."

I shook my head. "No, even if you didn't give

them the codes, they would have found a way to get in and destroy us—that's apparent after everything we have been through. Byron was always a step ahead of us, although he definitely wasn't a step ahead of his brother. But nonetheless he always has a backup plan on top of a backup plan on top of another backup plan. If he didn't use you, he would have gotten to your parents somehow. Or maybe he would have just used another Kausian to disable the shield. There were many options—"

Cor interrupted me. "But I gave in. There is still that fact, Ellie. I was the one who agreed to it."

"To save your own life. You trusted someone and they used you. You are not to blame—you were just a tool that Byron used and threw out."

Cor let out a slow breath. "Ellie, you don't understand. It's not just the codes... I did a lot of things to try to get close to Krax. I... was a bounty hunter. I killed innocent people."

I turned to him and made him look me in the eye. "You aren't the only one who was a bounty hunter. Zach and I have done things that we will never be able to atone for in this life as well, but we had to do it to survive just like you had to. We were even about to kill Gabe, and the only reason we didn't was because we found out he knew where you were. His blood would have been on our hands. And we both can agree that Gabe hasn't done anything to deserve a bounty on his head, and who knows how many others were in the same boat that Zach and I turned in or killed."

Cor didn't say anything for a moment, then turned away. "I know you are trying to make me feel better, but I'm still just so... I don't know. I should be grateful I still have you. And Gabe. I should be happy, but I don't feel like I deserve it. I didn't deserve you all rescuing me. You should have left me. I should be rotting in a cell right now."

I slapped him across the face, which I regretted as pain shot through my bullet wound. It was worth it though. Cor stood there for a moment, stunned.

"Are you an idiot? We saved you because we care about you! What part of we all have sins we have committed don't you understand? Stop being a martyr and do something to help the world, or don't. It really doesn't matter at this point. We all are just trying to save our skins. We have been through a lot—way more than any of us should. Just…" I took a deep breath. "Know that we will have your back. We get it and nothing can change the past; we can only choose our future."

He took all I said in for a moment then leaned in and kissed my cheek. "That means a lot, Ellie. Thank you. I'm glad out of all the people that you have forgiven me."

I blushed a little. Although I had wanted to kill him at one point, learning why he was sneaking out and taking lessons from Byron broke my heart all over again. He wanted to get into a university so he could give me a better life.

What would have happened if Byron had been truthful and honest? What if Cor had gone to a university and was able to get a nice job? Would we have been happy? Would we have still been together? Could we have made it in this crazy world?

Would we have been happy?

I wanted to be with him, but I felt guilty that Gabe was still passed out in the structure we would now call home. The discussion about our feelings wasn't going to come up anytime soon. I knew that as a fact. I watched as Cor appeared to be lost in thought. He was staring down at me, watching my every movement. It made my cheeks blush even more.

"What are you doing?" I asked.

He came back to reality and kissed my cheek again. "It's nothing. Now, do you want to tour the frozen lake, or do you want to go back inside?"

I was tired, but I had been lying down for far too long. "The frozen lake would be nice."

"Okay, let's go."

Cor led me down one of the trails that was apparent Zach and Cor took frequently as there was a carved trail from frequent trips. He nodded to the plant life. "This area will be good for harvesting. We have some hawthorn trees, walnuts, acorns, crab apples, and there is some watercress next to the lake. We will have to be careful harvesting to make sure we don't take too much for next year, but luckily we don't have to worry about other people harvesting. Just us."

A lot of those foods could be dried and kept all summer, so at least we had that going for us.

"We can also do some ice fishing, I think, and it's cold and dry enough for us to freeze-dry it all outside. But we do have to be mindful of bears. And make it bird proof."

If it wasn't one thing trying to kill you, it was definitely another. "How much ammo do we have? Just in case."

"Not enough, but that's always the case, isn't it? I mean, we found a rifle and a few rounds for it in that abandoned shack, but I'm not sure how long that would last us if we went hunting."

At least we had something other than our revolvers. We can use the rifle to keep us safe against the animals or for some meat, and the revolvers we could keep just in case some bandits found us.

Cor added, "Should hopefully last us at least a winter. Maybe. If we're lucky."

"Well, you know us—the four luckiest people

alive."

He let out a brief laugh. "You got that right. But we have survived this far, which I think luck had to have some part of why we are still kicking."

We arrived at the lake, and I stared out at the ice sheet. It almost appeared like glass over the water. I wanted to walk out on it, but I had no idea how thick it was. It was almost always cold here, however, so chances were it was quite thick.

"It's been a while since I have seen snow and ice like this," I commented as I took a deep breath of the cool air. "It's beautiful, but I know I'll regret saying that in a few weeks' time."

"Yeah, we will definitely be cursing this place if we survive."

"We can always leave if we need to."

"Yeah, but where would we go? Everyone wants us dead."

That was a good question. Our faces were going to be plastered everywhere. Yes, we could leave, but we were going to be blamed for every bad thing that was coming. We had nowhere else to go. We had no home, no family, no friends. It was just the

four of us against the world.
    I had never felt so alone.

CHAPTER IV

Gabe

The scene played out in front of me like some sort of vision, or perhaps it was a memory? I wasn't sure but all I knew was that I saw a younger version of myself—a child of only three or four— smiling and laughing as I held my mother's hand. I peered up at her with the happiest face I had ever seen myself have. She appeared majestic with her long blue dress and her black hair up with golden pins. On the other side of my child self was a man with short blond hair and in a dark blue suit with dark brown pants. He also smiled, but it was not like my mother's smile. His was fake. It was as if he were forcing himself to act as if he were happy.

That man was my father. I was sure of it. He didn't come to visit me often, but I knew he had when I was younger. This must have been one of those times. I looked so happy because I didn't know the truth. I didn't know what his plan was and how he was going to use my mother. How he was going to use me.

We all had been fooled.

I tried to reach out toward the scene. "Mother, please listen to me! He isn't the man you always claimed to be!"

But she didn't hear me. This had to have been a dream. Or, perhaps, I was dead. Did my uncle or father finally kill me? Did my luck finally run out?

No, I could feel others out there watching over me. It had to be Cor, Zach, and Ellie. They were keeping me safe wherever I truly was. This was just a nightmare—the same nightmare that kept playing in my mind each and every night. I just had to wake up and I would be fine. That is, if you could call reality fine.

The scene changed to a banquet. All the Sirian officials and politicians were there. I watched as my sister ran by. My heart felt as if it were going to leap out of my chest.

No, not this scene again. I do not want to see it again.

My mother stepped down the stairs and addressed her people as I watched from the crowd. I tried everything I could to close my eyes, but it was no use. This form wasn't obeying my command. I was not in control.

And I had to watch my mother be killed by a Kausian disguised as myself. The entire hall went into chaos, and everything moved around me as I stared at my mother's body, blood staining her dress and pooling on the glass floor around her.

This wasn't fair. None of this was fair.

The scene changed once again and this time it changed into darkness. So much darkness. It was cold—icy even. Where was I? What was going on?

What had happened?

My eyes flickered open, and I found myself somewhere I didn't recognize. All I could see was wood, cloth, dirt, and moss. I didn't see any windows, and the only light that lit up the area was from a burning fire in the center of the room. There was some kind of makeshift funnel that led the smoke up into the ceiling, if one could call it a ceiling. Even with that, it still smelled like smoke inside whatever building I found myself in. Even with the fire right in front of me, I could feel cold air on my skin.

I moved a little, and pain shot through my body. I grimaced and kept trying to move.

"Whoa, whoa, whoa. Don't move. You have been unconscious for a while now."

It was Zach. Relief swept over me. If he was with me, then it was fine. That meant Cor and Ellie were somewhere as well and we were safe. Or at least somewhat safe.

But as to how I got here and why I was unconscious, I wasn't sure.

"What happened?" I asked as he tried to help me

sit up. "Everything is a blank. How did we get here? Where exactly are we?"

Zach's eyes widened, as if surprised that I could not remember, and then appeared a bit sorrowful. That wasn't good, I thought. We must have been in more trouble than I realized.

He finally answered. "We're in the mountains. We had to make a run for it."

"From Byron? Did he do this to me? Seems like something he would do. Did he use some sort of poison? What exactly happened?"

Zach opened his mouth and then closed it again. He fluffed the makeshift pillow I had and got me up. "We have some food. You need to eat to get your strength back up. I have stew going with some berries, leaves, and a little meat we were able to get. Don't ask me what kind of meat."

It was probably a cute critter then. I tried not to think about it, as I could tell there weren't going to be any other options. "That would be great. I'm pretty hungry, actually."

Zach went to the fireplace and scooped some soup out of the cauldron that was hanging over it.

Even though I knew on any other day it wouldn't be as delicious as it smelled, at that moment it seemed like the best meal in the world. I must have been out for quite some time to be this hungry.

"So Cor and Ellie are around as well?" I asked.

He nodded. "Yeah, they are."

I tried to push back any jealous thoughts I had about them being alone together. There was only four of us, of course at times it would just be the two of them.

"I presume you want Cor to tell me what happened?" I asked as Zach brought the bowl over to me.

"I think you should get some food in you and relax a little. What happened happened and telling you everything if fine now isn't going to help."

Turning my attention to the soup, I tried to keep my expression neutral, but I knew my face was full of worry. If it were Byron, Zach would have just said so. No, something else happened. Something that Zach didn't want to bring up.

I took a sip of the soup, and it was simple yet very satisfying. Although it was sort of sour, I enjoyed it. I downed the bowl in no time flat and it helped bring me a little more energy. Hopefully soon I would feel myself again.

"So where did Ellie and Cor go?" I asked as I handed Zach the empty bowl.

Zach shrugged. "Good question. I was getting some stuff for this soup, and when I got back, they were both gone. I assume Ellie woke up and wanted to move around, so Cor took her outside."

"Oh, did she pass out too?"

Zach shook his head. "No, she got shot. Nothing new for her, so don't worry about it. She just lost a lot of blood in the beginning, so she was a bit weak. She's getting better now. Just a little stir crazy, which is probably why they went for a walk."

"That's good to hear. She seems like she is a tough cookie."

Zach laughed. "You could say that again. She's been shot quite a few times. It's a wonder she can keep moving like she does. I have a feeling when she gets older, it's going to bite her in the ass though. All the stuff we've been through will come back to haunt us one way or another."

I knew he wasn't just talking about physical wounds. I had done things I wasn't proud of to save my life or a friend's. But my life was in jeopardy, and I had to make a choice.

After I finished my soup, Cor and Ellie came into the makeshift hut. Cor's eyes widened when he saw me sitting up.

"Gabe! You are awake!" Cor quickly helped Ellie inside and made his way over to me. He knelt down next to me. "How are you feeling? Are you hungry? Did you eat?"

I smiled at all his questions. I could tell he was worried. I would have been as well if the roles were reversed. "I'm fine. Zach got me some of the soup. I just… I don't remember what happened."

His brow furrowed. "You don't remember what happened to you?"

I shook my head. "No. I mean, I kinda remember going to help you and Byron was there, but that's about it."

"Do… do you remember who else was there?"

I glanced around. "Zach and Ellie were there…"

I tried to get the memories to come forward, but it was all a mess. "I feel like someone else was there. Someone important?"

Cor glanced at Ellie and Zach as if they were trying to communicate without words. I felt as if there were a knot forming in my stomach. What was I forgetting? Who could have been there that was important?

"Please tell me what happened. I need to know. None of you like to have secrets kept from you, and I promise if you were in my shoes that I would tell you the truth. Now please tell me what happened."

Turning his attention back to me, Cor sighed. "You were poisoned by something that only affects Sirians. It didn't affect us or who we were having dinner with… We were able to make you throw up, and it didn't affect you as bad as it could have because you are only half-Sirian."

Poisoned. So that was what happened. I still felt like they were leaving something out, however. "Okay, that makes sense as to why the past few days have been a blur. Thank you very much for saving me and keeping me safe, especially all the way out in the mountains. But who poisoned me if it wasn't Byron?"

They glanced at each other again. Cor let out a breath. "Let's back up a bit. Do you remember us getting thrown into prison?"

I nodded. "Yeah, and then Byron captured you when the rest of us escaped and so we went to save you. That's about when it gets hazy."

"Do you remember how you got into Byron's house?"

I tried to think back. How did I get into Byron's house? "I mean, Byron's house in the Human Zone, right? That would mean…"

It felt as if a dam had opened up in my mind and all the memories came back. My father had done this to me. My father acted as if he had wanted to help—he acted as if he had been bothered by mother's death. But he hadn't been. It was all part of some sort of plan.

Then he tried to kill me.

"You remember, don't you?" Cor asked.

I wiped away the tears that were forming in my eyes. "Yeah. I do."

Ellie patted my leg. "I'm so sorry, Gabe. I didn't see it coming either. None of us did. He was a monster in disguise. I wish we could have killed him right then and there."

I didn't know what I wanted. He was my own flesh and blood. He was my father. Byron had always said my father hated me and was just using me, but I never believed him. Apparently, he was right.

My childhood fears and insecurities were all flowing back to me. Did anyone care about me, or were they all just using me to get what they wanted? Did these three actually care? Were they really my friends? Or did they need something and then were going to dump me somewhere?

I shook off the thought. No, if they didn't care, they would have abandoned me long ago. I couldn't imagine how difficult it would have been for them to move me out here unconscious, not to mention Ellie was injured as well. If they didn't care for me, they would have left me there and saved only Ellie.

"Do you want to be left alone, or do you want us

to stay here?" Cor asked. "We can give you a moment to process everything, or we can stay here and give you whatever support you need. Or a bit of both."

I smiled a little. A lot of people thought Cor didn't care about anyone but himself, but he was actually quite thoughtful in situations like these.

"I think I need a little time alone to process everything. Then I'll be back to my old self." I gave a half-hearted smile. "I promise."

Zach patted my back. "Take all the time you need. We'll go gather some more stuff and scout the area."

"Thank you."

With that, the three of them left, and I found myself all alone again. I wrapped my arms around my legs and began to sob.

CHAPTER V

Zach

I could hear Gabe as he began to cry when we shut the door. My heart ached in my chest, as I assumed Cor's and Ellie's did by the look on their faces. He didn't deserve this. None of us did.

We didn't deserve our home being destroyed. We didn't deserve being hunted down like animals because some guy decided to take it personal that we wanted to stop him from destroying all the world. We didn't' deserve getting chased out of all the towns and now had to survive in this treacherous place.

Now we were alone with no place to go or other friends or family that could help us. But at least we had each other. It was a miracle that all of us had survived this far and for that I was at least thankful.

"I'm glad he remembered on his own," Cor commented. "I did not want to tell him the truth."

I glanced down. "Yeah, me neither. That was why I waited for the two of you. I'm glad he was able to piece it together, but it's going to take some time for him to accept all that happened, if he ever does. I wouldn't blame him if he didn't. It's not easy when your own kin betray you and wish you were never born."

Ellie put her hand on my shoulder but didn't say a word. I wasn't exactly accepted by our kind either, a lot like Gabe. At least I had the two of them to stand up for me while Gabe had no one growing up. It was still hard though as many people commented on how I shouldn't have existed and wished something terrible would happen. Although my mother loved me, it was even hard for her to look at me sometimes. And like Gabe, I couldn't blend in in my own home as my red hair stood out amongst all the white and black haired Kausians. Red hair was a sign of being half human and all of them could easily target me for their bullying.

But that didn't matter now. They were all dead.

I felt guilty thinking so poorly of those who had been killed in the attack from the Silurians. Ellie and I were lucky we made it out alive but only because Cor was involved with the attack and got us to leave town without telling us the truth. I didn't know if I could forgive Cor completely for everything that had happened, but I knew I would have probably done the same thing in his position.

In fact, I had done the same thing. I was the one who gave the orders to kill all those Silurians up on Zynon. The thought made me sick to my stomach. Krax had been the one who gave the orders to destroy our kind. We had faced so many prejudices from the Silurians that it made me feel they weren't so innocent, but that didn't mean they all deserved to die.

No. I couldn't blame myself. It was all Byron's fault. He forced me to transform and give the orders or he would have killed me and Ellie. He forced Cor to do what he did as well with probably the same threats—killing Ellie or his family. Byron would do anything he could do to have his way, and he didn't care who was in his way. All this destruction and death was on his hands and his brother's. We just got caught up in the middle.

And now we were letting him destroy the rest of the world.

No. I couldn't think about that any longer. We had to save our own skin. We had to stay alive and hiding all the way out here was the only way to survive. The entire world had turned their backs on us. They didn't care if we were all killed—in fact they were always all quick to turn us in. They could save their own zones and people if they really cared about justice. No, they would probably just let him win just like they let him destroy our people and let him set up the Silurians and start a war with them.

"Should we take a walk. Again," Ellie asked. "I don't want to just stand here."

And hear him cry. I knew that was what she meant and to be honest I didn't want to hear him cry any longer either. Cor and I nodded, and we began to head toward the woods. All of us had now ventured out here a couple of times, but it was at least a nice stroll, for now. Once winter came, it wouldn't be as delightful.

"I wish it would stay like this all year," Ellie commented. "I do enjoy the snow, or at least this light snow where there is just a couple of inches covering everything almost like a blanket."

"I agree," I said. "It is beautiful and almost peaceful. And quiet. No nosey gunmen, no one trying to kill us, or at least not up here."

"Just the mountain itself," Cor added.

I sighed. "Just the mountain itself."

The trees swayed in the wind and a bit of snow fell on top of Cor's head and slid down the back of his neck. He let out a bit of a scream.

I pointed and laughed at him. He frowned as he grabbed some snow in his hands and quickly formed it into a ball and threw it at me. It hit me straight in the face.

"Oh, you asked for it," I exclaimed as I grabbed some snow. Ellie stepped out of the way, laughing, as her arm was still recovering and neither of us wanted to cause her any harm.

I pelted Cor in the stomach, and, in turn, he threw a couple my way. The first one I was able to get out of the way for but the other hit me in the face again.

"You two better stop or you are going to hurt each other," Ellie said between giggles. "There will be plenty of time for more snowball fights when I am all healed up and can destroy both of you."

Cor and I eyed each other, seeing if the other would give up. We both dropped our snowballs.

Cor turned to Ellie. "Don't forget Gabe."

"I wouldn't destroy Gabe, just you two."

He smiled. "Well, I guess I will use him as a shield."

Ellie rolled her eyes. "I will still win, so don't even think about it."

I watched as the two of them made googly eyes at each other. I let out a bit of a sigh. Were they going to ever stop flirting? I did not look forward to that love triangle thing blowing up in their face —especially since we were all stuck out here together.

Ellie turned away from Cor and peered around. "If only it stayed like this all year, then perhaps this place wouldn't be so miserable."

Cor shook his head. "No, that would mean this place would be habited and we wouldn't have somewhere to hide."

That was fair enough. "Some people have lived out here. Supposedly."

"Those stories always involved someone heading off to the mountains to never be seen again. The people telling those stories like to think their loved ones are still alive, but the odds are that they are dead somewhere. Like whoever was living in that hut we found earlier," Cor commented.

I shrugged. "I don't know. Maybe that person went back. Maybe we should have stayed there."

"No." Cor was quick to respond. "The building was too close to the bottom of the mountain. Odds were someone could find us there."

"Bandits hadn't found it," I said. "Otherwise we

wouldn't have found those supplies."

"You guys—" Ellie began.

Cor cut her off. "Why have you been arguing with me every step of the way?"

"Because you try to act like you are the smartest person here and don't let anyone else give any input!"

"You guys," Ellie said a little louder this time, but Cor and I were in too deep now.

"Because I know how to survive!" Cor exclaimed.

"You guys!" Ellie yelled. "Shut up! There's someone up ahead!"

We were silent as we turned to where she was pointing. Sure enough there was a group of people. Cor was quick to pull out a knife.

"What should we do?" Ellie whispered. "They outnumber us. Did Jonathan send people after us? Are they bandits? I didn't think bandits came all the way out here."

"They don't," Cor answered. "Odds are they are working for Jonathan."

I shook my head as I tried to examine them, but

they were still too far ahead. "No, they look like they are gathering wood. Why would assassins or whatnot be gathering wood? Wouldn't they just try to find us as quickly as they could and kill us?"

Cor and Ellie frowned. They knew I had a point.

"So, who are they?" Ellie asked. "Are they on the run as well? Are they in hiding?"

"The better question is, are they a threat?" Cor sighed. "I don't want to go up against them right now, but I also don't want to leave them to find us and gain the upper hand. If they find our hut, they could plan an attack while we're sleeping, kill us, and take what little supplies we have."

"Or maybe there is another one behind you and has heard your entire conversation."

My heart felt as if it had jumped out of my chest. All three of us spun around, and we saw the last person we ever thought we would see again.

Ellie was the first to speak. "Brother?"

Ellie's older brother Edmund opened his arms wide. "My sweet Elvira."

Ellie was quick, even with her wounds, to run into his arms. He squeezed her tight, and I watched as tears filled both their eyes. To be honest, tears were filling my eyes. How was he alive? And what was he doing out here?

"Edmund. I can't believe you are alive," Ellie whispered. "How is this possible?"

Ellie's brother was alive. I peered toward where the group was. Were they also Kausians who survived? More of our people had survived?

Cor stepped back. His eyes were wide, and it appeared as if all the color had left his skin. He was as white as the snow that surrounded us. Ellie's brother and Cor hadn't gotten along when they were younger, but I had a feeling that wasn't why he was in shock. No, he was afraid they knew the truth. He was afraid they would blame them for the destruction of our kind and that they will kill him.

Ellie and I only knew of Cor's involvement because he'd told us to run and then he disappeared. We knew he had known what was about to happen, and that was why we figured he was responsible. But whether these Kausians knew the truth, I had no idea.

Edmund took a deep breath. "There were sirens.

Some of us were on the edge of town and ran. We were able to save quite a few Kausians. We have a whole settlement just north of here."

A settlement of Kausians? The tears began to run down my face—cold and clinging to my skin. Our people were alive. How did we not hear about them? Why were there no rumors that a whole settlement of Kausians had survived?

I rubbed away the tears. We had met other Kausians before, but they were all Kausians who had already been living away from the zone. They weren't people we grew up with like these people were.

How many were there? Was my mother still alive?

I had a feeling she wasn't since she didn't typically go to the outskirts of the town. We had lived in the center—right where the bomb had hit. I would wait to see, as I didn't want to hear the truth quite yet. I wanted to be happy that Ellie's brother was alive. I wanted to find happiness in this moment.

"I can't believe it. There are others that

survived." Ellie stepped back to look at her brother. "I'm so happy, Edmund. For far too long I had thought you were gone. I never could have imagined..."

"And I can't believe you are alive. I thought for sure you..." He trailed off. "It doesn't matter. We have found each other at last." Edmund glanced up. "And Cor and Zach made it out as well. This is fantastic."

I saw the relief rush to Cor's face. Either he hadn't heard of how the Silurians were able to attack Kaus or he was trying to earn Cor's trust and then turn him in so the others can torture him later. Either way, he was safe for now.

"We have another," Cor commented. "A friend we ran away with. He isn't Kausian, but he is half-human, half-Sirian and is an outcast."

Edmund seemed to consider this info. "I don't have a problem with it… But…" He glanced down the path toward the other Kausians. "I'm not sure how everyone else will feel about letting an outsider in. I'm not sure if they will let any of you in. We have strict rules to not be found out." He glanced to me and then turned back to Ellie.

I knew that look. He didn't want to say it out loud, but I was considered an outsider to all of them. They had never accepted me, and by the way Edmund was acting, they never would.

But that was fine with me. I had Ellie, and she would always be there for me. She trusted me. She knew I would never betray the Kausians. And yet there was still a sharp pain in my chest.

CHAPTER VI

Cor

I wanted to run. I wanted to run as fast as I could in any direction.

But these Kausians couldn't know the truth of what had happened. They'd left everything behind and hadn't been in contact with anyone for the past three years, or at least that was what I gathered. They couldn't know the truth—they couldn't know I had caused the destruction of Kaus.

Or perhaps they did, and these would be my last few moments. Perhaps they would take me to whoever was the leader now, and they would execute me in front of everyone. Just like I deserved.

No, I couldn't think like that. I had to act calm—I had to act like I was glad to see everyone. Ellie's brother was always suspicious of me. He would pick up on my guilt, and he would start interrogating me. Just like old times.

Glancing at Zach, I could tell he knew what thoughts were running through my head. He didn't say anything, however, as he was dealing with his own anxiety. The Kausians weren't the kindest to him growing up. No—they saw him as an outsider. Ellie and I were the only ones who were his friends, and Ellie would beat up anyone who bullied Zach, which was why no one was friends with her. With how Edmund was acting, it was clear that they weren't going to be too happy with Zach joining the settlement, let alone Gabe. I couldn't blame them for being overcautious with Gabe, though. Not after what had happened, even if it was one of their own people who had betrayed them. But they didn't know that—they thought it was purely the Silurians.

But they never had to treat Zach the way they did when we were children. He was just a kid—what could he have done? He couldn't control who his parents were.

I turned my attention to Ellie. She was over the moon that her brother was alive. I was happy for her even if her brother and I didn't get along. In fact, he had threatened me quite a few times when we were younger. He was very protective of Ellie, and well, I was considered a bad influence.

He wasn't wrong. But that didn't mean I didn't love Ellie and that I wouldn't go to the ends of the earth for her. Edmund didn't know I had tried to go to a human university. No one did. That was part of the deal that Byron made me agree to. That way no one knew he was the one behind it all and no one could warn me about him.

The guilt felt as if it were going to overcome me as Edmund stood in front of me. But I couldn't tell them the truth. They would kill me, even if I had been tricked. I had no idea they were going to destroy the town—I had believed they would just go in and take it for themselves. Had I known the truth, why would I have told them the codes? Or would I still have protected my life and Ellie's? Part of me knew the answer.

No, I had to keep quiet and pray that none of them knew the truth or questioned the fact that the Silurians were able to disable the shields. Perhaps they thought it had been a malfunction or they had been able to sneak in. There were a lot of theories that could have been deduced if one really knew how the system worked.

"Come." Edmund motioned to us. "We must discuss with the others what to do."

Which meant he didn't know if they would let us in. Or, I should say, they would let us all in. I had a feeling Ellie would be let into their group without a problem. Zach and Gabe would be the ones they would have some issues with. And me—well—that depended on what mood they were in and if they knew what had happened that day.

However, if they knew anything, Edmund would

have been the one to end my life. He wanted any excuse to get rid of me so Ellie would marry someone else. He would have been happy to do it, and he definitely had the weapons on him to make it quick.

The question was, would I be able to stay with them without the voices in my head calling me a murderer every second for the rest of my life? And what if another Kausian from the outside found this little tribe they had going on? What if they told them everything and they killed me on the spot? I would be living in constant fear.

But hadn't I been living in constant fear already? Hadn't I already been on the run from everyone? Including Ellie? And what if they started asking whether Ellie and I were together? How would I explain this complicated love thing I had going on with her and Gabe? And how would Gabe feel being the outsider in a situation like this?

And what if they decided to let us in but not Gabe?

I wasn't as positive as Ellie was when it came to living out in the mountains. I honestly didn't think the four of us would make it. But with a group as large as Edmund suggested and the fact they had been out there for three years, we would be fine. But if they didn't let Gabe in, we would have to stay with him, right? It wouldn't be wrong to leave him behind.

Yet something in the back of my mind would rather save my own skin, and I didn't like it.

Had I always been this selfish? Had I always put my needs in front of others? I had risked everything to give Ellie the life she deserved, but had I really done it for her, or had I lied to myself and wanted to have a different life than what my parents wanted for me? I was supposed to take their place in securing Kaus, but I didn't want that. I wanted to see the world or at least what I could, and I wanted to leave Kaus. But Ellie wanted the same, didn't she? We had snuck out so many times, I assumed...

I shook my head. It didn't matter. We were well past that. Now Kaus was gone, and we found ourselves on the run because practically every zone was against us. Well, Byron had made every zone against us. If they had known the truth, perhaps they would be on our side.

Edmund took us to the others who were hunting and gathering with him. There were a total of seven Kausians in their party, and I wondered how many were part of their settlement or if this was it. And I wondered who was alive. I doubted my family was alive since they would have been manning the shields—of which didn't work and was hit by one of the bombs.

"Claude! Sam! Come and see who I found!" Edmund called out to the two closest Kausians.

Although the three of us normally didn't hang out with many others our age—or anyone really—everyone knew everyone in Kaus. Claude was the son of a blacksmith and had dark curly hair. He was Ellie's brother's age, so about four years older. He and Edmund had been good friends and spent a lot of time at Ellie's house. I had a feeling Claude had a crush on Ellie, but he never acted on it. If it were up to Edmund, he would much rather have his best friend be his brother-in-law than me.

The other man, Sam, who had hair as white as snow that was now much longer than he used to have it, was a loner and kept to himself more often than not. He did odd jobs here and there, mainly for the post office or any other place that needed deliveries.

Both men made their way toward us, brows furrowed as if confused anyone would be out here, which was fair. We weren't exactly expecting to run into anyone either.

"Elvira?" Claude gasped as his eyes appeared to sparkle. "What… how…?"

Yeah, he definitely still had a crush on her. I watched as he wrapped his arms around her and twirled her around just like Edmund did. I held back any comment I wanted to make. She wasn't my fiancé anymore, and they had both thought each other dead.

So why did I feel the sting of jealousy? Perhaps because I knew Ellie deserved better than me? That she deserved someone like Claude?

"I'm so happy you're alive. I feared the worst," Claude said as he set her back down.

"And I feared you all were gone as well. I can't believe you have been out here this whole time,"

Ellie said as he set her back down. "How many of you are there?"

"A little over fifty," Claude answered as he glanced to me. "Cor, Zach, you are alive as well. What luck."

I had a feeling those were empty words, or at least they were to me, but I gave him a smile. "And I'm glad you all made it out as well. I can't believe so many were able to escape. If only we had known, we would have searched for you."

"We wanted to go and search for more Kausians, but we feared if we left the mountains, our location would be found out. There are parties that go down for supplies, but we don't make ourselves know. We have to keep those we have in the group safe. You understand."

We all nodded. We understood things had to be done in order to survive.

"But you have found us," Sam commented. "Even when we were hidden."

"By pure luck," Ellie said. "We're hiding from, well, a lot of people. We decided to make our way into the mountains. We had no idea you all were out here."

"So you led people out here?" Sam asked. "After we have spent so much time staying out of trouble."

I didn't like where this was going. Ellie shook her head. "They didn't follow us. No one is stupid enough to look for anyone out here. The person who was after us has no idea where we went and won't be diverting manpower to this area. Not when he needs it all for what he is doing…"

"What do you mean?" Edmund asked. "Who is after you?"

"It's…" Ellie glanced at Zach and me. "Complicated. I'd rather discuss it sitting down somewhere. You can either come back to our camp, or if you are willing to let us stay with you, we have a friend who needs medical help. He was poisoned, and I think he's on the mend, but you never know. And there is also my arm."

"You've been through a lot." Edmund took a deep breath. "We can take you to our camp, but I'm not sure how people are going to react to your friend."

"We can blindfold him," I suggested. "You can blindfold all of us, and then people can hear our story. If they don't want to keep us there, you can blindfold us again and leave us in the middle of the mountains somewhere. Does that sound fair?"

The three of them glanced at each other when Edmund finally nodded. "Yeah, that sounds fair. Let's do that. Now show us to your friend."

CHAPTER VII

Ellie

My brother was alive.

Never in my wildest dreams would I have ever believed that Edmund was still alive. Who else was in their camp? I wanted to ask, but I also didn't want to seem that I cared about some people's lives more than others. I wanted to know if Cor's parents were alive or Zach's mom, but I had a feeling neither would be. Cor's parents would have been working on the shields and trying to get them back up when the Silurians attacked, and Zach's mother, well, she spent most of her time at the bar and was never coherent enough to walk straight. Zach spent many nights helping her back home.

I doubted our parents were alive either since Edmund didn't say anything. I felt it would have been the first thing he'd say to me, but he hadn't said either way. It hurt too much to ask even if I had already mourned their death. The pain was still there—deep down. It never truly went away. I could feel it waiting for an opportunity to resurface, and it felt as if I had lost them all over again. I didn't want that feeling to come to the surface right now—not when I should be happy about finding my brother.

But that also made the tears flow freely down my face.

Edmund helped me as we headed toward the makeshift camp where Gabe was still resting. Claude and Sam followed us as well, half to make sure everything was fine, and probably half to make sure we wouldn't do anything to jeopardize their settlement. We weren't trusted by our own people. I understood, but it still hurt.

I knew my brother trusted me, but he couldn't speak for his entire community. At least I would have him on my side. But if he found out about what Cor had done, would he think I was also responsible? Would he be mad that I hadn't told him the truth of what happened? I could let them know, though. I couldn't let them take everything out on him. Cor had only done what he did to survive. He couldn't have known the truth.

Glancing back at the others, I watched Claude and Sam. They seemed so different and yet seeing them almost made it feel like it was just yesterday we were all at our house, having dinner, and goofing off. I could almost hear my father and mother's voice scolding me for not eating my vegetables. But we could never go back to that time. All of it was gone in a blink of an eye.

It was strange to see Claude after all this time. He and my brother had been good friends, and he was almost like another brother to me. I could never see myself with him, even after he told me how he felt. I never told Cor that he confessed to me, and after that night, both of us acted like nothing had happened.

Sam and Claude were pulling up the rear while Zach and Cor led the way to our little shack, so Edmund and I were in the middle. He kept shaking his head as he helped me along.

"I just… I can't believe you are alive. After all this time… If I had known."

"You couldn't leave the camp. I understand. Zach and I tried to live in the wilderness. There are a lot of bandits out there who like to raid and attack, not to mention so many people don't like Kausians and use any excuse to attack."

"You and Zach? What about Cor?" he asked.

Right. They didn't know the truth. They didn't know what he did and how he was responsible for Kaus's destruction. Well, not so much responsible as much as tricked. Any Kausian that wandered the zones knew of what happened as rumors spread. Were those rumors started by me? Perhaps. Perhaps Cor's actions also added to those rumors since he was working for Krax. Either way, that information hadn't made it all the way out here.

Otherwise, they would have killed him on the spot.

"We got separated after the attack," I said a little louder than I had been speaking so Cor could hear what story I was giving so we could keep it all straight. "I didn't know he was alive or he I until, well, a couple of weeks ago. But, uh, well, three years have passed, and Cor has a boyfriend now."

I watched as my brother glared at the back of Cor's head. "So he broke your heart."

Cor probably could feel my brother's eyes on him, but he ignored it and didn't turn around. I didn't blame him.

"No, it's not like that. He didn't know… I didn't know. We just… We moved on."

"But you still love him, don't you?" my brother whispered. "Even after all the times I begged you to leave him. Even after all the times I threatened him."

I punched my brother in the arm. "I don't need you trying to pick who I am or I'm not with. I can take care of myself, thank you very much."

"Clearly. You survived the world for three years with Zach. I can't imagine what your life was like."

I didn't know what all I wanted to tell him. There were so many things I would never have imagined doing—things I didn't want Edmund to know about. I had to do them in order to survive, so I didn't feel guilty in that sense. But I just… I didn't want him to know how bloody my hands truly were.

"We'll talk later," I whispered. "Okay?"

He nodded, understanding a lot had happened. While he and the others had dealt with the physical environment of the mountain, we had completely different environments to endure.

"So I take it Cor's boyfriend is the half-Silurian?" Edmund asked.

I nodded. "Yes, and he's really kind and openhearted. Too much, if you ask me. Especially after everything he's been through. I hope the others will let him in and listen to what we have to say."

"I hope so too. But you know how some Kausians can be. Especially after the attack. We have been isolated for three years, Elvira. I'm not even sure how they're going to feel about the three of you coming into the camp, let alone a non-Kausian."

Although I understood their thinking and how they wanted to stay safe, it did hurt a little that my own people might not accept me after all this time. However, could I really stay there and live a simple life in hiding like that? Did I have a choice at this point? The entire world felt as if it were after me. I had a feeling Jonathan had his hands in more chaos and pockets than Byron did. He just let his brother do what he wanted until the time was right.

Jonathan wanted Byron to do all the work for him, and then he would step in and act as if he were taking revenge. Instead of destroying everything, however, he was going to try to rule it all. The first place he was going to take over was the Sirian Zone by avenging Gabe's mother and helping Gabe's sister take command. He would tell her some load of bullshit to win her over when really he had set it all up since he first met Gabe's mother. It was all so disgusting.

"Just… get the others to hear us out. Then they can decide."

"I'll do my best, li'l sis. But I can't make any promises."

I had finally gotten my brother back, and I might not even get to be with him that long. We might have to part yet again, but at least I would know he was safe. At least I could have hope for the Kausian race.

We made it back to the shack we were staying in. It was quiet and I wondered how Gabe was going to react seeing a bunch more people. He probably wouldn't be too worried since they were Kausians, and we weren't tied up and such. It was clear this was voluntary.

Cor opened the door and stepped inside. He kept the door open so Gabe could see all of us. He sat up in his bed, his eyes red after probably having cried the entire time we were gone. Gabe asked as he glanced between the three of us as if trying to deduce whether we were in trouble or not. "Uh, what's going on? How did you find people all the way out here? Are they with my father?"

"It's all right," Cor said not very convincingly. "They are Kausians. They are friends."

I knew Cor was thinking some people were more like friends than others. But he wasn't going to say that out loud. Not with Claude standing there. The two of them didn't quite get along, not to mention my brother and him did not get along at all.

"This is my brother Edmund. A group of Kausians survived the attack and have been living out here for the past three years," I explained.

Gabe's eyes widened. "Your brother? Really?"

I nodded. "Yup, can't you see the resemblance?"

Edmund and I turned so our backs were together, and we posed dramatically. It was something we always did because, to be honest, we didn't look that much alike unless you really examined us. But we definitely could make the same oddball face.

Gabe laughed. "I definitely see it now."

"We are going to go up to their camp and tell them everything that has happened to us," Cor explained. "Zach and I will help you."

Gabe glanced between us all again, as if wondering if this was a set up, but he knew there was no use in protesting even if he felt threatened. He wouldn't be able to survive down here on his own. He nodded. "All right."

I noticed Cor was lying yet again. We weren't going to tell them everything because everything meant we would have to tell them about how Cor was the one who gave them the codes. Although my brother and the two others didn't seem to want to kill Cor at that moment, it was possible someone knew something about it. Then we would have to either talk it all out or we would have to run for our lives.

Or perhaps only Cor would have to run for his life and pray no one would ever catch up to him. It wasn't as if all of us should be held accountable for what he did. I let out a slow breath, hoping my brother wouldn't notice my worries.

I couldn't let Cor run away again—not when I'd spent so much time trying to find him. We had a lot more to work out between what happened three years ago and the kiss just days ago. I still believed he was my soulmate—my twin flame—but seeing Gabe with him, I couldn't deny they also had a connection.

Glancing out the door to where Claude stood, I couldn't help but think about when he had slept over one night and in the morning told me he loved me and asked me to leave Cor and date him instead. I told him that I could never do that to Cor, and he never brought it up again. But now with things so complicated, perhaps he and I could pick up where that left off.

Turning my attention back to Cor and Gabe, I knew that wouldn't work out. I had given my heart fully to Cor, and there was no changing that. Claude deserved better than me. I watched as Cor smiled at Gabe.

But what if Cor didn't feel the same about me?

CHAPTER VIII

Gabe

I couldn't believe there were Kausians all the way up here. Was this where they all were hiding? How had they survived? I had so many questions, as I presumed Cor and the others did as well. The Kausians were probably also curious how we got up into the mountains and why we were hiding here. We would have to tell them about my uncle and my father, which I assumed wouldn't be to our advantage. Would they think I was helping my father? That this was all a ruse to get them to trust me? I couldn't blame them for wanting to protect themselves—not after everything that had happened. Not after everything my family had done. At least I knew Cor, Ellie, and Zach were on my side and that they would speak up for me.

"Are you ready?" Cor asked as he held out his hand to help me up.

"Yeah, I might be a little slow, though. My arms and legs feel very tight after being unconscious for so long."

And they truly did. I felt like I was some sort of statue coming alive. Everything hurt and I struggled to move. I wanted more than anything to feel normal again. You never appreciate feeling perfectly fine until it is taken away from you. I hoped these side effects would go away soon.

Cor and Zach helped me up and out of the tent. Ellie and her brother quickly grabbed what supplies we did have and put out the fire. She was still moving slow, but Ellie seemed to be moving fine. I felt guilty as she had almost died because of me. If

I hadn't dragged them to my father's—if I hadn't told them they could trust him she would be fine. Everything these people suffered through was because of my own family. How would they ever forgive or trust me? I was putting the possibility of them being accepted into the settlement in danger.

What was I going to do?

There were two other Kausians with the group. They seemed fine enough, but they didn't really say anything. They sort of stared at me with suspicion. I couldn't blame them—they probably haven't seen anyone since they ran away from the attack, let alone someone from a different race.

After the others were ready, Ellie's brother Edmund nodded to us. "We are going to have to put something over your eyes for part of the journey just to be safe. We don't want anyone knowing our location."

We all nodded. That made sense to me. I wouldn't want to jeopardize their safety. I just hoped they would hear me out and listen to my story. Even if they didn't accept me, perhaps they would let the others stay. I would be fine with that

—they deserved it.

But then why did part of me feel like they were abandoning me? Just like all the people had in my life?

I knew that wouldn't be the case. I knew that they would try everything they could for me to be accepted into the settlement. With everything that has happened, it was clear they cared about me. I needed to not let childhood traumas affect my friendships and relationships now. I needed to stay in the present moment.

Cor helped me along as we ventured into the wilderness. I knew it would be cold outside, but I never could imagine how cold it really was outside our shack. I had never been anywhere that was this cold before, and I wondered if I would ever get used to it.

Sirians were not built for cold. The sea was quite warm, and the structures we built were always kept at a moderate temperature. Even when I was on land with Cor, we stayed in areas that were typically warm or were moderate in temperature. There was sometime some rain, but never snow like this.

"I'm just realizing," I commented to Cor. "That this is the first time I have ever seen snow."

Cor glanced around. "I wish it was under better circumstances for you. Snow can be quite fun when you play in it."

"Play?" I asked. "Like how?"

He shrugged. "I don't know, like snowball fights, sledding, building snowmen. Those sorts of things."

I didn't know what any of those things were, but it sounded fun. "Perhaps later?"

"Yeah. Perhaps if the settlement accepts us, we can do stuff like that. Or if it doesn't, I guess, since we will be living here on our own. If they don't kick us off the mountain."

Or kill us, is what it felt like he wanted to say. I couldn't imagine them kicking us off the mountain, but I couldn't exactly imagine them letting us into the settlement. I didn't want us to have to build our own homes in this climate—I doubted we would survive the winter—especially if it was this cold and still summer.

We were able to walk quite a while without the Kausians blindfolding us. I was thankful for that as I didn't know how well I would be able to wander around without being able to see, even with some help.

I took a deep breath as I peered up at the sky. Soft snowflakes fell onto my face. Snow was beautiful—I had to admit that. We would see if I'd say the same thing in a few months. I'd probably grow to hate it.

I still felt weak from the poison, but I could tell I was slowly getting my strength back the further I walked. Ellie walked with her brother in front of us. They definitely seemed similar, even if they didn't quite look the same. They both had a strong aura to them, and I had a feeling Ellie looked up to her brother when they were younger. He seemed like a good lad and inspired her to be strong herself. I wished I could have had someone like him to look up to when I was younger.

Edmund stopped and nodded to the other two Kausians. They pulled out some cloths and put it over our eyes. One of the Kausians took over for

Cor helping me while the other one led Zach and Cor. Edmund still helped Ellie along after she was blindfolded as well.

Thirty minutes went by, and I thought I was going to collapse from exhaustion. Perhaps I wasn't doing as well as I had hoped. I was glad someone was helping me as I could tell he used more strength to keep me up so I wouldn't have to do much of the work. We finally stopped and the Kausian took my blindfold off.

As my eyes adjusted, I found that were in front of a cave. The cave was boarded up with wood, ice, and snow. It appeared that there were two layers before one could enter the cave, which would keep it insulated more. I glanced over to my three Kausian friends. They appeared as impressed as I was. I had known Kausians were resourceful, but no one had ever survived in the mountains this long before—at least none that had ever come back to the cities and told the tale.

There were a handful of Kausians sitting on the outside, watching us closely. One of them waved to Edmund and approached him. She was tall with dark hair and golden eyes. She wore a lot of layers, but I could tell she was quite muscular by her build. I would not want to mess with her.

"You are back early. Who are these people?" the guard asked.

Edmund nodded to us. "We found some Kausians hiding on the mountain. They have nowhere to go, so we are going to bring them to Mae to tell her their tale."

She eyed us. "You know you aren't supposed to bring others into our camp."

"I had to. My sister was among them."

The guard started to open her mouth but then closed it. She motioned to pass, and Edmund led us into the settlement.

As I had noted, there were two sets of doors, but even as we entered the first set, we found it was quite warm inside already. There were guards between the two walls, and they nodded to Edmund to proceed.

There was a lot of security for this place. It wasn't as if there was anyone else out here. But I could understand their worry—they didn't want their people to be destroyed again.

The inside of the settlement was like that of a quaint marketplace. There were small, makeshift buildings that were probably homes and storage. Dozens of Kausians were wandering around, hanging clothes to dry, gathering food, and interacting with one another. When we stepped in, the area grew quiet as everyone stared at us.

It had definitely been a while since they'd seen strangers.

Well, I supposed since Kaus was such a small zone, they all probably remembered Zach, Ellie, and Cor, but I was a complete outsider. I wasn't someone any of them would want to trust. I was the only true outsider to them.

Maybe coming here was a bad idea.

Cor grabbed my hand and squeezed it. I had a feeling he was as terrified as I was about all this—not only for my life but also his own.

Did any of these people know what had happened all those years ago? I had a feeling if they did, Ellie's brother would have shot him on the spot. I hadn't even known, and I had been with him for a while.

"Let's talk with the head chief first," Edmund commented as he led us past all the people that stared. Even I could tell he was uncomfortable with all the eyes that were on us. "She should be around here somewhere."

Edmund led us through the makeshift town, and eventually he found who he was looking for. The woman was tall, elderly, and had short white hair. She was helping a couple with the siding of their home as it had rotted from the moist air that filled the cave. I wondered how often they aired it out as they probably wouldn't want the cold air coming in, but they probably also didn't want to deal with the possible mold.

The woman turned to us as we approached. "Edmund, I see you have brought us some guests. If I remember correctly, Elvira, Zachariah, and Cornelius."

The three of them nodded. Ellie responded. "Mae, correct? It has been a while."

"That it has. I mainly remember the three of you because you were always such troublemakers." She glanced to me. "And I see you brought a friend."

Edmund spoke up before Ellie could say anything. "I can vouch for them for the time being. I feel they have quite the story for us. I figured you would want to speak to them first."

She eyed each and every one of us with her golden eyes. "You assumed correct. Let's go to the meeting hall."

The woman led us through the labyrinth of houses to the back of the cave. The only light was from oil lamps. We arrived at a room that had a large table and chairs all around. She sat down.

"Okay. Let's hear it. Why are you all here?"

CHAPTER IX

Zach

I recalled seeing this woman when we were growing up. She had been on the council for as long as I remembered. She was one of the few people who tried to stop discrimination against half-Kausians such as myself, not that it did any good. People were set in their ways, and they didn't care if such actions hurt innocent lives such as myself, and Gabe for that matter.

"Mae Carter, it has been a long while," Ellie said with a smile. "It doesn't surprise me to find you in charge. It's no wonder you all survived out here for three years."

Mae didn't smile, which wasn't saying much. I didn't remember seeing her smile often when we were growing up, but most people didn't smile back then. There was too much hardship in our world.

Mae responded. "It wasn't easy. It took a lot of time and effort from everyone to put this settlement together. As you probably guessed, not many people survived the attack and those that did are here." She gestured around. "We are but a fraction of what used to be."

"Of course." Ellie lost her smile. "Many lives were lost that day. In fact, I didn't even know this many had survived. I thought it had only been those who were not in Kaus during the bombing, but they had been so far removed from Kaus that they didn't try to come together to start a new settlement, not that I blamed them. Any attempt to make another settlement would have been quickly squashed. Other than up here, of course. No one could have known about this settlement."

Mae leaned forward. "Which brings me to the question, how is it that you found our community? Don't get me wrong—I care for each and every one of you. But I have to keep this town safe from outsiders. We won't let what happened to Kaus happen to us again."

This didn't sound promising. I kept my mouth closed as I knew I wouldn't be the best to try to talk Mae into letting us stay. Even if she did stand up for me often when we were kids, I doubted a half-Kausian like me would be able to talk her into letting us stay.

Ellie glanced at Cor for a second, then she turned back to Mae. "I agree, I don't want anything like this to happen to the Kausian people again. However, we bring information on who was truly behind the attack. It was a human by the name of Byron Hill. He tricked the Silurians into attacking Kaus. He and his family were the ones who planted the seed of doubt in all the zones about our people. Then, when the time was right, he destroyed our kind. Then he started a war with the Silurians and caused the Sirians to close their borders so he can destroy all the other races and let humans reign over Mu."

Mae tapped her fingers on the table. "And what does that have to do with you four?"

It had everything to do with us know. I wasn't even sure how to explain it all to anyone who hadn't been there. I noticed Cor begin to open his mouth. Was he going to confess that Byron tricked him? There was no way.

"Well, we sort of keep getting in the middle of his plots," Ellie explained before Cor could say anything. "We keep trying to stop him from hurting innocent folk, though we haven't been successful. On top of everything, though, Byron's brother Jonathan murdered him and is now trying to rule over all the nations and suppress all nonhumans."

Mae seemed to be digesting that information. "I still don't quite understand how that had led you to my doorstep and why I should trust this outsider here." She nodded to Gabe. "If it were just the three of you, I would have no quarrel. It would have taken some time to convince the others, sure, but they would have agreed that you three wouldn't betray us. But I cannot trust outsiders. Not after everything that has happened."

Before Ellie could respond, Gabe spoke up. "I'm the son of Jonathan and the Sirian queen. I was a pawn in his game to take over the Sirian Zone. My mother was murdered by Byron, and he set me up to take the fall. My nation wants me hanged, and my father wants me dead. These brave Kausians took me in, even when it almost cost them their life. I would never do anything to betray their trust —not after how many times they have saved me."

Gabe shifted a bit as the leader of the town examined him closely. I wondered if she was going to kick Gabe out. Would we stay if that were the case? I didn't want to turn my back on Gabe, but this was our people; this was where we belonged. There was no way any of us would survive out there. Too many people were after us, and I doubted the four of us could build a camp good enough to survive the winter—not like this. We were better off staying here where we had friends and family. Or at least Cor and Ellie had friends and family and I had them.

Were any of my extended family still alive? Not that they wanted me in their life anyway. They had kicked out my mother after she married a human and then that human had left her. It wasn't as if I had any friends besides Cor and Ellie. Everyone picked on me due to me being half-human. It wasn't as if I'd chosen my parents. I couldn't help who I was. But if Ellie chose to stay here, I would stay by her side. She was everything to me—even if it meant I might have to deal with those people all over again. It wasn't as if any other places were much better.

"So, you are half-Sirian then, correct?" Mae asked Gabe.

This question caught me off guard, just as it probably did Gabe. He quickly nodded. "Yes, I am."

"I have witnessed how half-humans are treated, even in a place like Kaus." Mae's eyes flickered to me. "I know you tell the truth and wouldn't bring destruction upon our town; however, I can't guarantee that others will feel the same. I can't guarantee welcoming arms for any of you, in fact. You will have to present everything to the council, and we will put it to a vote after some discussion. But you may stay for the time being as long as you follow the rules. I presume Edmund can give those to you. As for a place to stay, we don't exactly have any spare homes since no one comes and goes, but we can build some new ones in the coming weeks, if the council approves of you."

"They can stay in my place," Edmund commented. "Might be tight, but I can stay with Claude for the time being until we build them something."

Mae nodded. "Well, then, I guess that solves that. Edmund, show them around and give them a list of the settlement rules. I'll talk with the other elders about my decision. I will send for you when they want you all to present your case."

I wasn't looking forward to having to present our case, but at least we had somewhere warmer to sleep tonight. Perhaps they would accept us like Mae had, but I wasn't going to hold my breath. Now we had time to plan for a plan B.

Edmund led us out of the meeting hall and back into the labyrinth-like town. Although in a cave, there was quite a bit of light from the lightbulbs that lined the top of the cave. I assumed at night they dimmed them all to make it appear like evening. A lot of the structures were in styles that the City of Kaus had, which of course made sense given who was building them. It felt almost nostalgic in a way.

Where they got all of these supplies, I wasn't sure. Where was the electricity coming from? Was there some sort of generator? Did people go into town for supplies, even if they acted like they didn't? Perhaps there was more to all of this then they were letting on.

We passed by a few Kausians who stared at us, wondering what exactly we were doing there. I didn't know if I should say hi or keep walking. I stayed close to Ellie and decided to do whatever she decided to do, which was usually ignore everyone around and yet pay close attention. I wished I could be as confident as she was walking through a town.

"The washroom is over there." Edmund pointed. "And the communal kitchen is over there." He nodded in the other direction. "We take turns with chores. It has been running pretty smoothly thus far —a group of people do all the laundry for the town, then a group does the cooking, so on. Then we all switch chores. The only people who don't necessarily have to do chores are our two doctors and Mae since they have their own specialized tasks, but when they don't have much to do, they usually help out, as you saw with Mae when we first found her."

Edmund weaved through the buildings. "We also take turns going out and foraging. The stronger of us hunt or at least those of us who know how to use a weapon. Sometimes we can be outside for a few days, so you have to be strong and willing to endure the nights in the summer. They can get quite cold."

"That we have already figured out," Cor commented. "But for a cold climate, there are quite a lot of plants to eat around aren't there?"

"We were surprised about that too. If one knows

how to handle the cold well, we have found that this place isn't as uninhabitable as the stories tell. That being said—the shed you were sleeping in wouldn't have survived the winter."

Cor nodded. "Oh, we knew that. It was just for us to use until Ellie and Gabe got better."

"Right. I'll have our doctors come check out Ellie's wound and Gabe. But by the looks of it, both of you are on the mend it seems."

Gabe and Ellie nodded, and Ellie said, "Yeah, it isn't as if a bullet to the arm is anything new for me."

Edmund glanced at his sister. "What do you mean?"

She shrugged. "I had to make my way through the world somehow. Zach and I became bounty hunters. It wasn't the safest of jobs, but it sure paid well."

Ellie's brother's face filled with worry. I could tell there was a lot he wanted to say, but this wasn't the time nor place. "Well, you won't have to do that any longer. You are safe here." He turned. "Speaking of which, here is my home you can stay in for the time being."

It was quaint, just as were all the buildings in this little town. There was a bed, a desk and chair, and some shelves for miscellaneous stuff. I wasn't sure how all four of us were going to sleep in here, but I wasn't going to argue.

"I'm going to let you rest a little and fight over who gets the bed first. I will find some sleeping bags for the rest of you. If you need anything, I'll be next door that way." He pointed. "Which is where Claude's home is."

The door shut behind Edmund, and I let out a long breath. We were finally safe.

CHAPTER X

Cor

There was no way this was going to end well.

I was already feeling claustrophobic—and not because we were in a cave. There were a lot more people here than I thought there would be, even if it was just a fraction of what our home once was. One of them had to know the truth. One of them had to know it was because of me that all their lives were in ruin. With all these supplies that they had, they must have gone to different towns. I didn't believe for a second that they created all this on their own. Which meant they interacted with others, which meant there was the high chance they ran into someone who told the truth that happened. Told them I was the one responsible.

Granted that wasn't the whole truth, as Byron had tricked me, but that didn't matter. These people lived in a cave because of me. These people lost their loved ones because of me. I shouldn't be here. I had to get out of here.

Ellie grabbed my wrist before I could turn to face the door.

"Don't you dare," she growled.

She was always two steps ahead of me, which made it a miracle I was able to evade her for three years like I had. She was going to make an escape difficult—I could tell that right then.

I shook my head. "I can't stay here, Ellie. You know that."

"Yes, you can. We all can. They don't know what happened. If they did, you would already be dead and you know that."

"What if they find out the truth later? What if something happens?" I asked.

"Then we will deal with it when the time comes. Where else would you even go? You have the same threat no matter where you go. We will be safe here. No one knows about this place so when war breaks out, we will all be fine. We can wait it out—see what the damage is in a few years. Maybe the world will come back to a balance."

I let out a defeated laugh. "A balance? Ellie, it has been years since they attacked our nation, and there has been no balance. In fact, the world is worse off than it had been. There is no way this is going to resolve itself in our lifetime."

She shrugged. "Then we stay here. This is where our family is, Cor. This is where our people are, and they clearly know how to survive."

Cor shook his head. "No, your family is here, Ellie. Your brother is clearly the only family that's alive and if you haven't noticed, we don't exactly get along. There is no one here for me."

Ellie frowned. I shouldn't have said that—I knew. She was here and that should have been all that mattered but I couldn't help but notice my family wasn't here. Staying here would be a reminder that they were gone. Because of me. All these people were suffering because of me.

Zach held out his arms. "Let's just… rest for a bit. The council will call upon us later. We need to give them details of what is going on in the zones. And we have to keep our story straight so none of us seem at fault."

I gave him a look. "You mean so it doesn't look like it is all my fault."

He shook his head. "I didn't say that. We all have dirtied our hands in a way. Byron used me as well to start a war with the Silurians. But it is none of our faults. We all were pawns in a game that we will never win. You understand? We can't run any longer."

I glanced at the ground, trying to calm myself down. That wasn't true—they hadn't dirtied their hands. At least, not as much as I had. "I'm surprised you would want to stay, Zach. You know they are going to treat you like shit, right? You'll be an outcast here just like you were in Kaus years ago."

"That's enough," Ellie said before Zach could respond. "Cor, go sit in the corner."

I laughed, thinking she was joking. She pointed and snapped her fingers. I sighed and went over and sat in the corner and sat down, cross-legged. I was facing away from them, so I didn't know what her reaction was. "Happy?" I asked.

She ignored my comment. "Zach and Gabe, how about you two rest? I'll hang out with Cor and make sure he doesn't do anything stupid."

I turned and stuck my tongue out at her, and she did the same in retaliation.

Gabe and Zach shrugged as they climbed on top of the bed. "Fine, whatever," Zach commented. "I'm not that tired, but I'm sure Gabe is."

"Yeah, it's almost as if being poisoned can mess with your body."

The two of them lay down, although I had a feeling they weren't going to actually sleep. Ellie took a seat next to me and just stared at me. After a few moments, I sighed.

"What?" I whispered.

"Why do you keep running away from all your problems instead of facing them?"

I gave her a look of annoyance for calling me out like that, but she had a point. I had been running away from all my problems because, well, what else was there to do? It wasn't as if I could go back to the way things were. I couldn't have the life I wanted for her.

I shook my head. "I don't know. I just… I can't keep feeling like I need to get away, Ellie. I just can't. It's as if… I want to run back to how things were, but I know I can't which makes me want to run even faster."

"It's sure easy to rest with all this talking." Zach's voice came from the bed. "I'll definitely be able to sleep."

Ellie rolled her eyes and then reached out her hand. "Come—let's go sit outside. I'm sure my brother wouldn't mind as long as we stay next to his house."

We moved outside and sat against the house. I let out a sigh as I watched people wander around. People seemed familiar but I couldn't put names to a lot of the faces. Was that because I didn't really know them when I was younger or was it because I didn't want to remember the names of those whom I hurt? It was easier that way.

I clutched my knees into my chest. I didn't want to be here. This was a mistake. I should have ran the moment I saw Edmund. He probably wouldn't have gone after me as he didn't want me near Ellie anyway. He would have been happy to see me instantly disappear.

Ellie placed her hand on my knee. "You know we're here for you, right? We have your back. We came for you when you were captured by Byron. You can't just… run. Okay? I don't think I have it in me to try to hunt you down again."

I grabbed her hand and squeezed it. "I don't expect you to come find me, Elvira. You deserve better than me. You should just… you should just move on."

She shook her head. "Don't even say stuff like that. I made my choice a long time ago. If I wanted someone better, I would have left you way before all this happened."

I let out a laugh. "What, and go marry Claude or something?"

She snorted. "He would have loved that."

"Ah, so you knew about his feelings for you."

"It was obvious. And he confessed to me one night a long time ago. I turned him down, of course. It was when we were getting really serious."

I hadn't known that. I thought he had backed off because we were a couple and was just waiting for when we broke up. I didn't realize he had the balls to confess while Ellie and I were together. It wouldn't have been before since she would have been just a child. We had been together since middle school.

Jerk.

"Ah. You never told me that. Well, I bet if you asked, he would want to pick up where that all left off. I saw the way he looked at you out there. He still cares for you."

She turned and looked at me in my eyes. "Are you saying I should? Are you saying we're through?"

I was silent. We were both silent. I opened my mouth, but no words came out. I didn't want things between us to ever end, but I never imagined I would have Ellie back in my life. It wasn't as if I had moved on—I had simply found someone to try to fill in the hole that was my heart. I could never replace Ellie, but that being said, I couldn't exactly turn my back on Gabe either.

"I don't… I love you with all my heart, Ellie. But I also…"

"Love Gabe," she said matter-of-factly. It wasn't as if she said it with hatred or with sadness. Her voice was just void of feeling.

She turned back to face the area in front of Edmund's house, and I did the same. We watched as people passed by, glancing at us but never approaching. Had our arrival already gone through the rumor mill? Did they know we were some outsiders that Mae had agreed to host until the council decided?

Of course they knew we were outsiders—they all knew each other in this settlement. The information about Mae letting us stay for the time being also probably went through the rumor mill since people would be curious about why there was new people.

So far, I didn't see any family—not even extended family. They had lived near the middle of the city, so it made sense. Ellie had lived on the outskirts on a farm. Now that I thought about it, it seemed like most of the people I recognized were farmers. It made sense given their location.

They would have been further from the blast and would have had enough time to escape.

I wondered if Ellie's parents had survived. I felt that Edmund would have said something if they had—or, at least, I knew it would be the first thing I would have told my long-lost sister. But at least Edmund escaped the attack, even though he hated my guts. I couldn't wait until he found out about the love triangle Gabe, Ellie, and I had found ourselves in. He would deem me not suitable for his sister, not that he ever had. He would probably be thrilled if Ellie and Claude ended up together. And perhaps they should. Claude was a nice guy— a lot nicer than I was. She deserved someone who wouldn't leave her like I had.

That day would haunt my dreams forever. Every time I closed my eyes, I saw the explosion. Every time I wanted to move on, I got dragged deeper into the mess that I had caused. And I was dragging everyone down with me. I was responsible for all of this and now I had to see it with my own eyes.

But did none of these people really know the truth? Did no one know it was I who had destroyed everything we had grown to love? I was the one who gave the codes?

Only time would tell.

CHAPTER XI

Ellie

He was going to make a run for it the moment I looked away. I could tell.

Call it woman's intuition, or call it knowing Cor like I did. He always ran away from his problems even when we were kids. If he got something wrong in school, was in trouble with some teachers and stuff like that, he would ditch class. It took me a while, but I figured out his hiding place—the woods just outside of Kaus. Anytime he faced some kind of conflict, I always knew where to find him, so I never really had to worry.

And it was the first place I looked when everything went up in flames.

Of course he wasn't there. I waited a couple days, kept checking back, but he never showed. It was part of the reason I knew he had something to do with what happened. If he wanted to find me, he would have returned to that spot. But the reason he didn't show was because he was running from me.

Where would he run off to this time? Would I be able to find him? Should I find him?

If he ran away again, knowing that I wanted him here, should I waste my efforts with him any longer? He made it clear I shouldn't—that I should stay here with my brother.

And for some reason that hurt me even more.

An hour or so passed, and Zach and Gabe woke up from their nap. I was pretty well rested already, and Cor was the same. We sort of rested anyway out here against the side of the small home that my brother had been living in for three years now.

It was strange to imagine he was alive here all this time.

I had mourned his death. I had moved on from it all, or at least I believed I had. Deep down, I probably hadn't but just suppressed all the emotions deep down. With every face I saw, the more I wanted to cry for those who did not make it.

But I didn't want to break down here. I didn't want to cry any more.

Cor and I went inside and all four of us sat around, the cool air feeling better here than it did out in the mountain. I had a lot to learn about this place and how it worked. Although there were problems with some of the wood rotting as we saw when we came in, the air didn't seem too stale or too humid.

"So," Zach said as he glanced around. "What do we do now?"

I shrugged. "I guess we just wait for my brother. I am not sure what else we have to do."

"Could always go through all your brother's stuff. I'm sure he would love it if we snooped," Cor commented just as the door opened. My brother stepped in and glanced down at him.

"Some things never change, do they Cornelius?" Edmund commented.

Cor cocked a grin. "Oh, you know me. I never learn my lesson."

Edmund sighed as he moved out of the way and let in Claude as well.

When I glanced at Claude, I wondered if Cor was right. Should I settle for him? It wasn't as if Cor would make up his mind anytime soon, if at all. Maybe I wanted security—maybe I wanted to settle down. Maybe I wanted someone who I knew would be there for me each and every day instead of looking for a way to escape.

Before my mind could wander on that thought, my brother grabbed my attention. "The council is ready to speak to you and hear more of what is going on in the zones. There will be food as well, so I hope you're hungry."

I had a feeling all of us were. We hadn't really eaten too much in the past few days. I was surprised I hadn't heard Zach make a comment about it. My stomach grumbled at the thought of food.

My brother smiled. "Once again, some things never change."

Zach's stomach grumbled even louder.

Edmund laughed. "Case in point. Now come on, we don't want to keep the council or the food waiting."

We followed Edmund and Claude back to the council room where the five councilmembers sat. They appeared as troubled as I thought they would as they stared at us, frowning.

Mae gestured to the seats across from them. "Take a seat. Food will be brought in here momentarily. We just wanted to go over more about what has happened in the past three years and what all you know."

Claude pulled out a chair for me, and I took a seat. He, of course, took a seat next to me, and my brother took a seat on the other side of me. This made me feel a bit isolated as I was used to being around Zach all the time. But I didn't argue. I hadn't been with my brother for three years, and it took everything inside not to cry every moment I saw him.

Because it was really starting to hit—my brother was alive. All these people were alive. Our kind had survived. At least for now.

"Now," an elderly man began. If I remembered correctly, his name was Melvin. "Tell us what exactly is happening in the zones."

I glanced to the others, wondering who wanted to give the details this time. Cor volunteered.

"There was a man by the name of Byron Hill, whose family has been weaving the webs of destruction for generations. They were the ones that made all the zones come to hate Kausians years ago. Then, with their influence, they urged the Silurians to attack Kaus." Cor paused, and I wondered for a moment if he were going to confess to helping Byron unintentionally. He went on. "Then he caused everyone to turn on the Silurians by setting them up to take the fall of a terrorist attack on Zynon."

"How do you know it was a setup? It's not as if the Silurians are an innocent bunch," Melvin commented.

Cor answered, "Because we were there and became Byron's target. We ran to the Sirian Zone in hopes that Gabe's mother, the leader of the Sirians, would help us."

Their attention all turned to Gabe. "You are the half-Sirian prince?"

Apparently they knew of him. I didn't know the Sirians had a prince who was half-human, but I wasn't much into politics as a kid or even now. I just kept finding myself in the middle of all the drama, however.

"I am. My mother was queen until she was murdered by Byron. She was going to help us take him down, but he already had the people on his side and used a Kausian to appear like me and murdered her in front of all her people."

"Was it one of you?" He glanced to the three of us. We all shook our heads.

"No, it was none of us," Cor answered. "After that, we ran and were arrested for some disastrous thing Byron had caused. The three of them escaped, but I did not. They came to my rescue at Byron's mansion, but then Byron's brother, who is also

Gabe here's father, killed Byron and is taking over the family business, so to speak. But instead of wanting to destroy all other races, he wants to rule over them all. We managed to escape, headed to the mountains, and that is when we ran into Edmund and the others."

The elders all looked at each other. Mae nodded. "That is what I told you all. What do you think?"

Melvin answered, "I think that it is all a lot more complicated than we ever could have thought of. I had always thought it was just our people that everyone was after. Never could I have imagined the web that this family has weaved."

"Right," another man commented. I was not sure of his name. "This is not what I could have imagined either. The rest of the zones will learn what it is like to be on the receiving side of all that hatred."

"And will you do something?" I asked. "I mean, the Lyrans might listen and want to help stop this takeover. We have enough people to stand up against Jonathan and his men. If we tell them the truth—if we tell them his plan—"

"No," Melvin answered before I could finish. "We will not take part in any action having to do with the other zones. None of them stepped up in our time of need. Why should we risk our lives for people who turned their heads during our genocide?"

I frowned. He had a point there. I knew that. But if we didn't do anything to stop Jonathan, he would get away with it. He would get what he wanted, and that didn't seem fair.

Someone else would have to stop him. It didn't have to be us. There were plenty of other people who could do it. The odds were I would die trying. I shouldn't have to give up my life for people who wouldn't do the same for our kind.

But why did I feel like we were hiding? Why did I feel like this wasn't the answer? Why did I feel like this was giving up?

Food was brought to us. It was mainly berries, mushrooms, leafy greens, and meat. I was amazed they were able to harvest all this and have enough to go around. They really had mastered the art of surviving out here.

We ate in silence, which was more awkward than it should have been. Usually people conversed over food, but that was not the case here. It felt as if they were watching us and if we did anything wrong, we would be thrown out.

Once we all finished our meal, the elders leaned back. Melvin stroked his beard.

"All right. I'll agree to let them stay. They have been through a lot and have brought us important information. As for the half-Sirian…" He eyed Gabe. "We will keep an eye on him, but I have a feeling he speaks the truth. I just can't guarantee how the community here will treat him."

It couldn't be any worse than Gabe had already been treated in the past. I glanced over to him. We would be here with him, so we could protect him from naysayers if need be. Besides, it seemed my brother had some sort of authority and could stop any rumors from going around.

"You will all need to start your fair share of chores, not to mention build a home or two for yourselves," Mae added. "Edmund, will you help them gather supplies and start in the morning? It shouldn't take too long to at least get a shelter up. Furniture may take a while. We only have a few carpenters in our mix."

Edmund nodded. "Of course. I can get them squared away and figure out where to start tomorrow."

Mae stood up. "Let us announce our decision to the settlement and stop any rumors that may be going around. I have heard enough comments throughout the day to last me a lifetime."

I didn't like the sound of that. After the council stood, we got up and followed. It seemed that most people ate in a community-style seating area in the middle of town. Although we had such community areas in Kaus, this was a bit livelier. There were people singing, dancing, eating, and laughing. I smiled as I took it all in. We had finally found our community.

That is, if they all accepted us.

As we stepped up, everything went quiet. I gulped when I felt a hand grab my hand and squeeze it. I turned to find Claude smiling at me.

"It will be fine. I promise."

I nodded slightly and turned back to the crowd.

"It has been quite some time, but we have some new members of our community, three of which some of you might recognize. Please welcome Elvira Rider, Cornelius Adams, and Zachariah Richards."

Whispers went through the crowd. I recognized some, if not all, of the people. They knew who we were—we were the three troublemakers growing up. We had made a name for ourselves, and it was then that I realized perhaps that wasn't a good thing.

"Lastly, we have Gabriel Pickett. He is not of our kind; however, I guarantee he'll fit in nicely here. Please remember, I would not let anyone in our community if I didn't believe them to be genuine and someone who would contribute to our society. If you have any concerns, please bring them to one of us. Now give them all a warm welcome."

The crowd was stunned for a moment, and I half expected them all to chase us out of the town right then and there.

Then they all stood and started clapping. Random

people came up to us and hugged us as if we were long-lost friends. I felt tears roll down my cheeks.

We were home at last.

CHAPTER XII

Gabe

I wondered if these people were really going to accept me, but where else would I have to go?

After the elders announced that we would be staying here, people came up and hugged all of us, me included. They welcomed me and said I didn't have to worry any longer.

The problem was I had heard that before. From my own father. Then he tried to kill me.

Could I really trust these people? They were welcoming now, but would they be tomorrow? Or if I was separated from the other three, would they gang up on me. Perhaps they were just happy now because they had a full stomach and had been singing and playing games. Then, come tomorrow, they would wake up and remember I was an outsider, and they'd do something to make me disappear.

I shook my head a little, trying to push back those thoughts. No, Ellie's brother and his friend had been nothing but kind as was the council. They listened to my story, which was less than most had given me for most of my life. Even my own people were quick to judge. The only people who had ever listened were Kausians. And yet they were the ones who everyone saw as monsters and attacked them. Did no one actually take time to get to know them? Did only fear control their judgement? It didn't seem fair.

To be honest, I hadn't heard of any one thing that the Kausians did to warrant people hating them. I had always heard about how they could transform and sneak into places, or how they could do this or that, but there was no one actual thing that they did to warrant any of this. It was all hearsay. It was all rumors that my family had put out in the world.

"Come." One person next to me grabbed Cor's arm. "Join us. We usually spend this time of day singing songs from our home. I'm sure you remember them all."

I followed Cor and the others as they got dragged down to sit with the townsfolk. I watched as Ellie sat next to her brother and his friend. It was apparent there was some history between her brother's friend and her. He was hovering a little, as if waiting for the right opportunity to talk to her about something. He probably had feelings for her. Ellie was an amazing human, anyone could easily fall in love with her, once they got past her scary exterior that is.

Glancing over at Cor, I found he was also watching Ellie and her brother's friend, frowning. I felt a piercing pain go through my chest.

Of course he would be wondering what was going on between the two of them—Cor and Ellie had been engaged. He must have known Ellie's brother's friend before the attack. Did this guy have an interest in Ellie back then as well? And now he sees that they aren't engaged any longer and is making his move?

I mean, I couldn't blame him. He had thought someone he loved was dead and now she was alive. I would confess my feelings if I were in his shoes —even if she was engaged.

The question was, did Ellie like him in return? I glanced back over at them. She definitely was smiling, but it wasn't the same smile she gave Cor. No, that was more like the smile she gave her brother. She saw him as family, I bet.

But why did part of me hope that she would end up with him? Then she would drop Cor and he would stay with me? That wasn't fair... but wouldn't it make the most sense? Wouldn't that mean it would be happily ever after for each and every one of us?

"Are you all right?" Zach asked as he sat next to me. "Are you still feeling sick?"

I glanced over to him and gave him a smile. "I'm

okay. I am just trying to figure out the entire dynamic here and how I will fit in. That's all."

Zach slowly nodded his head. "I get that. I am still trying to figure that out myself."

I was about to ask what he meant by that when people started clapping in a beat. Violins, concertinas, and guitars started playing and a few people stood up and grabbed a partner to start dancing.

Clapping, my worries began to vanish as I joined in with the music and sense of community these people had created. My heart raced, and I couldn't help but smile. I had no idea what the lyrics of the song was, but I did my best to fit in.

I watched Cor, Zach, and Ellie, and I had never seen them smile as much as they had at that moment. It brought a warm feeling to my heart that they felt like they belonged here. As long as I'd known Cor, and for the short time I had known Ellie and Zach, I could tell they didn't feel like they belonged anywhere. I knew that feeling all too well. I was happy for them, and so far, the people around us were welcoming to me as well.

It was mildly warm with everyone here like this, or at least it was warmer than the hut we were in. I was only completely conscious for a while in the hut, but I imagined it didn't get much warmer than it did during that time.

I had so many questions on how they set all this up and if they indeed went and got supplies or not. They said they didn't go back to the mainland, but I couldn't believe this was all done with supplies they already had.

After a couple of songs, Cor grabbed my hand and pulled me out to the center area where everyone was dancing. "Care for a dance, or are you not up for it still?"

I bit my lip. I indeed wanted to dance with him, but I could feel how weak my body was after how far we had traveled. I shook my head. "No, I better stay seated. I'm pretty tired."

Cor nodded. "I understand." He glanced around and I could tell what he was thinking.

"Go ask Ellie. It's fine."

He turned back to me. "Are you sure?"

I nodded. "Yeah, I'm sure. Go have fun."

Cor went over to Ellie and held out his hand. She smiled as she grabbed it and they went to middle of the dancing area and began swing dance. I glanced back over at Ellie's brother and his friend. Ellie's brother was frowning and crossed his arms. It was clear he did not like Cor, but his friend was frowning for a completely different reason. He was frowning as if he was sad or confused. It was clear he had feelings and wanted to dance with Ellie but hadn't worked up the courage yet.

This was going to end disastrous—I could feel it.

Ellie and Cor danced a couple of songs when Ellie's brother's friend stood up and went over to them. From where I sat, I couldn't hear what they were what they were talking about, but I could imagine he was asking if he could dance with Ellie. And by the way Cor frowned, I figured I was correct.

Cor came back and sat next to me. I didn't ask what happened and he didn't say anything. After a bit of pouting, he joined in on the clapping and singing. Zach patted his back but also didn't say anything.

Hours passed and people began to turn in for the night. I followed the others back to Edmund's place where we would be staying for the night. Hopefully by tomorrow we would have our own place and I wouldn't feel so bad about taking someone else's home. Before we approached, Edmund's friend took Ellie aside and spoke to her. Cor seemed to ignore this and kept walking.

"Wait, shouldn't we wait for Ellie?" I whispered to him.

He shrugged. "Claude is probably going to ask if she wants to stay with him and her brother. That way it would be less crowded, or some excuse like that."

Yup. He was jealous. "Does Claude like Ellie?"

Cor laughed. "That's an understatement. Worse part is that Ellie's brother likes him a lot more than he ever cared for me. He made that clear many times."

Perhaps there was more drama going on than I had realized. I wanted to ask for the whole story, but I knew this wasn't the time.

"Ellie's brother has always liked me, so there's

that," Zach interjected.

Cor gave him a look. I chuckled a little.

After a couple of moments, Ellie came back to the group. "I'm going to stay with my brother tonight."

"You mean Claude?" Cor replied.

She let out a breath. "Well, since my brother is staying with him, yes. But don't worry—I'm not sharing a bed with Claude, which is more than I can say for you these past three years."

With that, she turned back to her brother and Claude and went into the home with them.

Zach whistled. "She has you there."

"Yeah, well," Cor began as he turned to the home we would be staying in. "You are sleeping on the floor."

Zach gasped. "Hey, that's not fair!" he called after him. I chuckled as I followed them to the house.

Sure enough, Zach slept on the floor.

Edmund had pulled out a spare sleeping bag of sorts, so it wasn't as if Zach was just snoozing on the ground in his clothes, but it didn't seem that comfortable. Then again, he and Ellie had camped out in the wilderness quite often, so they were probably used to it.

I didn't sleep well, and I could tell Cor couldn't either. I had a feeling he was thinking about his fight with Ellie, and I was thinking about how I didn't like how much he cared about Ellie. Would the fact that someone else was interested make Cor leave me for her? Would he toss me aside and I would have to find a new life? Would I even be able to stay here?

These were all questions I didn't know the answer to. I needed to stop thinking about the future and start living in the present. Right now, Cor was beside me, and that was what mattered. The rest would happen if it was going to happen. At least I was safe and away from my uncle and my father.

There was no one here trying to kill me.

Morning came and there was a slight knock on our door. The door opened a crack, and the sound of Edmund's voice came into the room.

"You all awake?" he asked.

Zach sighed. "I am now. Is it breakfast time?"

It was good to hear Zach talk about food again. I hadn't heard him say anything about being hungry yesterday, and it made me worry a little.

He laughed. "You haven't changed, Zach. Come, there is breakfast ready in the common area. It's nothing fancy but will help get you ready for the day."

Edmund gave us some clothes we could change into, and we headed out to the common area. Sure enough, there were eggs and berries ready for us.

"Eggs?" Cor asked as he grabbed a plate. "Now where in this forsaken place did you find eggs?"

"We sent people down into the mainland a while back to get chickens and the like. They are held in a cave over from here and have been surviving quite well. It took a while to find what works for them, but we figured it out eventually."

They really had learned to adapt. I was quite impressed. I gathered some scrambled eggs and the berries and sat down next to Cor. People were intermingling, but it was apparent that different groups of people woke at different times.

"So did you sleep well?" Edmund asked as he, Ellie, and Claude sat down.

Cor picked at his food. "I didn't sleep that well."

"I mean," Edmund began, "you are all in a new place after all. It will take a while to get used to. And I'm sure you are stressed out. A lot has happened to you in the past day."

"Try a couple of weeks," Ellie commented. "All the stuff we told Mae happened in the past two or three weeks."

Edmund's eyes raised. "Really? Then you all must be really tired."

We all nodded. If I could sleep for a week, I definitely would. But I had to pull my weight around here. It was clear that this community worked hard to stay afloat. Everyone did their part, and I would do the same.

After we finished breakfast, we headed over to an area of the cave that was a bit sparser than the rest.

Edmund nodded around. "This will be where you all can start building. I can help lay the groundwork and with the layout. Then if you need any assistance after that, just let me know."

Ellie wrapped her arms around her brother. "Thank you so much for everything, Edmund. You are the best!"

"My pleasure. I'm just glad you all are okay and finally came home to us. Now let's go get the materials, shall we?"

CHAPTER XIII

Zach

It was hard work, but we were able to put up two separate buildings with the spare materials they had around the settlement. And by buildings, I meant the bare minimum to be considered a place to live. It mainly had a roof, sides, windows, and a door. But as long as we had some privacy, a cot, and a place to store our belongings, everything would be all right. We could wait for an actual bed like

Edmund had, or two for Ellie and me, along with some dressers and the like. It wasn't as if we needed them right away anyway.

The bathrooms were already communal, so that wasn't going to be a problem. As we found out that morning, there was a hot spring in the mountains that they tapped into and made gender-separated baths for people to wash up in. It was nice to soak in warm water—something I had missed in the last few days. Then there were restrooms that were kept clean and tidy. I appreciated that as we had had to do our business in some nasty places before.

The four of us had decided Ellie and I would take one building and Cor and Gabe would take the other. There were no objections, but Ellie and Cor had been quiet during the conversation and hadn't said more than a couple of words to each other. While I didn't exactly root for Cor, Edmund really hadn't liked him when we were younger. If I wasn't mistaken, they had gotten in a few fights over the years about Ellie and what was best for her. I wondered if that was why Cor had tried so hard to get a proper education, which then led to all of this.

I didn't know how I felt about whatever was going on between Ellie and Claude, however. He had been best friends with Edmund—almost like another brother to Ellie. I couldn't imagine her having actual romantic feelings for him. Was she just rebounding? Was she just trying to make Cor jealous? Who knew at this point? I was just going to mind my own business. I was happy we found a home and a place where we could belong.

And last night was fun—a type of fun I hadn't had in years. Although when we were younger, we didn't have many times where the whole town came together, but some communities like this existed, such as Ellie's family and the other local farms. They used to come together and have potlucks. It felt just like that. I never imagined we would have times like that again.

Because we had believed all these people were dead, and yet here they were alive and well. They had survived up here for three years, keeping each other safe and becoming a strong-knit community. And they all accepted us as one of their own.

Or at least it appeared that way.

Were the people who were prejudice against half-humans like me gone? Had they realized such prejudices would cause them all to die off? Or had they been so closed off from the world they would welcome anyone new just so they weren't stuck with the same people forever like they had believed? I knew I missed meeting new people similar to myself. Only time would tell.

But part of me felt as if everyone was staring at me—just as they had when I was a kid. However, when I peered around, I found that wasn't the case. Was it just my imagination? Or were they still wary of me because my father was human?

They hadn't seemed to care that Gabe was with us, which I found to be strange as well. He wasn't even Kausian and yet they accepted him as one of their own because he dealt with such prejudices. It made me a little jealous, if I were honest. They had treated me with such hostility, just as others had toward Gabe, and yet they gave him pity and ignored what they had done to me.

I couldn't let it eat at me, however. None of the people I recognized here gave me such animosity when I was younger, or at least I didn't think they did. Everything from back then was a blur. Then again, these people hadn't done anything to stop others from hurting me. Perhaps accepting us was how they felt they were going to make it right.

The day went by, and after we finished what we needed for the houses, it was already suppertime. The cave wasn't that warm, but after working all day, it felt hot, which was nice compared to how cold we had been for the past couple of days. Our people really had all this figured out.

"This reminds me when we worked on that home in the outskirts years before," Ellie commented. "Except this time we have help. And don't have to worry about bathing or bathrooms"

I nodded. "Yeah, a little bit. And at least no one is trying to shoot us this time around."

She laughed. "That was what I was thinking. But the night is still young."

I doubted there would be a shoot-out with anyone here, well maybe Cor and Claude, but I doubted it. If anything, it would be if Jonathan's men found us. I really hoped he didn't send people to the mountain to come looking for us. This place seemed secret enough, not to mention there were a few people always guarding this place. We weren't even allowed to know its exact location, although if we went to help forage and hunt, we would have to be shown a map eventually.

"How are the other two doing with their home?" I asked.

Ellie shrugged. "How should I know?"

I hesitated. "Do you want to talk about it?"

"Not particularly."

"This is a pretty small community—the two of you are going to be running into each other quite often."

She let out a breath. "I know. I just think the two of us need a little space from each other to sort things out. We will eventually figure it all out. We always do."

"Is that why you stayed with your brother last night?" I asked.

She glanced at me. "Nothing happened between Claude and me."

"I imagined it wouldn't have with your brother

there."

She smiled a little. "He is like a brother. I'm happy the two of them are alive and perhaps I wanted to be with my brother last night. It has been a while since the two of us have been under the same roof."

I glanced over at where Claude was working. He took a moment to look up from his work and smile at Ellie.

"Yup," I whispered. "Totally a smile that would be given to a sister and not one that would be given to someone they want to marry."

Ellie nudged me with her elbow. "Shut up. Just let me figure this out."

"Fine. Just promise me you won't do anything rash just because you are mad at Cor, okay?"

"I wouldn't. I don't feel that way toward him."

I let her get back to work as the two of us were almost finished with the door. I held it in place as Ellie put on the last hinge.

"Well, that's that," I commented as I wiped my hands on my shirt and pants. "Should we go find dinner?"

"You always think with your stomach, don't you?"

I grinned. "Always! I miss Kausian cooking. Everything tastes so good, and I always feel better after."

"Well then, let's go."

"Should we wait for the others?" I asked as I saw Cor and Gabe still had a bit to go.

Ellie shrugged. "They seem to have it handled. I doubt they'll be much longer. They'll catch up with us."

I glanced back and waved to signal we were leaving. As I did, Claude hurried over.

"Oh, Ellie, are you going to dinner?"

She nodded. "Yup! Thank you for everything you have done today. I wish there were some way to pay you. I would say I would treat you to dinner, but it is clear everything here is free, so to speak."

"Yeah, everyone just does what they can to survive. Don't need money in a community as small as this."

"Seems nice," I commented. "Ellie and I struggled here and there when it came to money."

"Oh?" Claude asked. "What exactly did the two of you do?"

"We were bounty hunters," Ellie answered before I could say anything. "We captured or even killed people for money. It was one of the few things Kausians could do to stay alive after our home was destroyed."

Claude was silent for a moment. "I thought you seemed a lot more… intense… than before. It must have been hard."

I snorted. "Intense is one way to put it. She definitely can outgun any of us here, even her brother now."

"So all those years going out back and shooting with your brother must have helped. You were always a good shot growing up."

"Had to get rid of all the rats in the barn somehow." Ellie sighed. "And most of the people we hunted were rats, so it all worked out."

Except for Gabe. It made me wonder how many people were truly innocent. I prayed that all of them were criminals one way or another except for him. And we hadn't hurt him, so it was fine. We didn't do anything wrong. We had to survive because the world took everything away from us.

"Well, here you can relax. We're all friends and family. We watch out for one another, and no one is going to try to kill you. And you don't have to worry about money any longer either."

I liked the sound of that, and by Ellie's smile I could tell she did as well.

We made it to where the dinner was being served and people were all seated at the communal benches, eating. Like yesterday, there were dozens of people simply hanging out and having a good time. This made me smile. Perhaps things were going to end up just fine.

The meal was similar to the night before, but I wasn't complaining. It was all delicious. I missed the spices we grew up with, but it didn't seem likely there would be much in the way of desert spices in the middle of the mountains. Whatever they used for flavor was still amazing, and I finished my plate before Cor and Gabe made it to us.

I noticed Cor hesitate to sit near Ellie, but there

was really nowhere else for him to sit without feeling more awkward. Although these were our people, there were still a lot of people we didn't know that well, and a lot had happened over the three years we had been separated. It almost felt as if everyone was a stranger except for Edmund and Claude, but that was only because he was Ellie's family.

Edmund grabbed his plate of food and sat down at our table.

"So," he began as he took a bite of bread. "What chores do you all want to sign up for tomorrow?"

We all glanced at each other. Ellie shrugged. "What are you doing tomorrow?"

"I'll be leading a foraging-and-hunting party. I'm one of the better shots here, so I usually am one of the people who go out and hunt."

Ellie grinned widely as she stuffed some bread in her mouth. "Oh? Best shot here, eh? I bet I'm better."

Edmund ruffled the top of his sister's hair. "Always so cute. But there is no way. You could never out gun me."

"How about a bet then? I bet I can shoot more beasties than you tomorrow. Loser has to, I don't know, cover a chore the other person doesn't want to do?"

"So just like old times? Of which, if you recall, I always won."

Ellie stuck her tongue out.

"I'll go with," Cor commented as he picked at his steamed greens. "I could use some fresh air. I can just pick berries or whatever. I don't want to get in the middle of this shooting match. I already know Ellie is going to win."

"I will join you," Claude said. "I can show you how we forage around here."

Gabe glanced at the two of them, as any of us could feel the tension in the air begin to rise. "I'll stay here. I'm not good with a gun anyway and I'm still a bit tired."

"I will stay with Gabe," I added. "Just to make sure everything is fine here. I'm sure Ellie will get enough food for everyone."

Edmund nodded. "Then it's settled. We will be in tomorrow's scavenging party."

CHAPTER XIV

Cor

It was cold out.

It had only been a little over a day, but I had already grown accustomed to the temperature of the cave. Joining the foraging group was a bad idea. I should have stayed where it was warm. There were plenty of chores I could have done inside—ones I could have done with Gabe. I could have just been content with that.

Who was I kidding? There was only one reason I came out here, and it was because I couldn't let go or be happy with what I had. Ever.

I took a deep breath of the crisp air. At least it was pretty outside. I walked behind Ellie and her brother as they playfully argued about who was going to be the better shot. Honestly, the best shot was probably Ellie. Edmund had been the better shot when we were younger, yes, but after the attack, shooting was all Ellie had, and I had a feeling she practiced a lot either to defend herself, finish a job, or just to practice for when she wanted to shoot me.

I strode through the forest next to Claude. It was just the four of us out today foraging and hunting. It was apparent that the settlement had a lot of food in storage but sent people out for extra food to add to the stock and to eat fresh as often as they could. One deer could feed the settlement for the day, and I imagined they would get a few deer a week at least, not to mention there were birds and possible other sources of protein in that cave they mentioned with the chickens.

They really did have it all figured out.

So what would my role be in all this? I supposed a lot of people had multiple roles in the settlement, but I felt as if I would be out of place—that somehow someone would put two and two together and know I had something to do with the attack. Would someone realize I wasn't with my parents monitoring the shields? Would they wonder how the Silurians knew the codes? Someone would figure out the truth, and they would come for my head.

I squeezed the basket in my hand. Claude and I were to forage berries and greens while the siblings found as many creatures as possible they could to shoot. I didn't particularly want to work with Claude, but I had no choice since he volunteered to help me. It wasn't as if I could ignore him in a settlement so small. And we were out here together.

He made especially clear he was still interested in Ellie. He saw that we weren't a couple anymore, or at least not technically a couple, and has been hinting for the past two days that he wanted to date her. Especially when he had her stay with him and

Edmund.

It made me angry, and I knew I shouldn't be. I had Gabe in my life, and if she went with him, then that meant I wouldn't have to choose. But that also meant I wouldn't be with Ellie. She was the love of my life—always had been. But Gabe was special to me too. It was all too frustrating, and I wasn't the best at sorting out my feelings.

"We are going to stop here and pick berries. This area hasn't been foraged in a while. We want to make sure there is still enough for the creatures that live out here and so the plant can survive for another season, so we make sure to change locations," Claude commented as he motioned to the berry bushes. "I presume you know how to tell if they are ripe?"

I nodded. "Yeah, we figured it out when Zach and I went picking. And these are similar in appearance to the ones that would grow along the streams in Kaus."

"I think those taste better, to be honest. Or perhaps everything seemed better back then."

I nodded. "Yeah, I get that. It seems livelier,

though. Here, I mean."

"Yeah, well, when you've lost so much, you try to push that sadness down by being thankful for the community you have."

"So it's like that every night?"

He nodded. "Yeah, or at least after a while. We got some instruments and started singing again. Partying. Trying to forget what happened and be thankful for those who survived. And to celebrate the lives of those who didn't make it out. We see it as a way to honor them. They wouldn't want us to keep suffering."

No, they would have wanted me to pay for what I did. I, of course, didn't say this out loud and turned to the berry bush and began to pick some ripe berries.

Claude and I didn't speak much and after a few minutes I heard the echo of gunfire followed by Ellie's voice. "Got one!"

I smiled. Soon after, there was another echo. Edmund's voice followed. "Mine's bigger!"

I shook my head. The two of them hadn't changed. After all these years and all the hardships, the both of them went through, they were still brother and sister and acted like they were still kids around each other. I wished I could go back like they could do. I wished all the blood that was on my hands would wash away by the smile of another. But that wasn't going to happen.

Because even though seeing Ellie happy brought hope into my heart, I still couldn't shake off the guilt I felt for everything I had done. And seeing all these people living how they had to… it was all because of me. I didn't deserve their hospitality, and they had no idea. I was an imposter, and I deserved to be hung for being a traitor.

"You all right over there?"

I turned to find Claude was next to me. I jumped a little as I hadn't heard him move from his bush over to me. The snow was sure quiet, and my mind was quite loud.

"Yeah, I'm fine. Just peachy." I turned back to the berries.

I could feel him examine me. "What happened?"

My heart felt as if it had skipped a beat. Did he know what I did? "Wh-what do you mean?"

"I mean with you and Ellie. What happened between the two of you?"

Oh. Right. Of course he would be wondering about that. I took a deep breath and shrugged. "We got separated during the attack. Both of us thought the other was dead until we ran into each other a couple of weeks ago. I began dating Gabe, and that was that."

"Ah. I see."

I turned to him. "So, what? Are you going to make your move now? Or should I say again since Ellie informed me you confessed your feelings to her when we were dating. Real honorable."

This probably wasn't the time or place to hash it out with this guy, but I couldn't take it anymore.

"Did she really just tell you that?"

"She did."

"So, she didn't tell you when it happened? Years ago?"

I paused. He had a good point—why didn't she tell me all those years ago? "Well, no. I guess she didn't."

"Interesting." Claude smiled a little.

It made me a little mad he was smiling about her keeping that secret. Actually, it made me really mad. I tried to take a couple deep breaths, but it didn't help. This was probably why Ellie didn't tell me years ago, but here we were, and I was still angry about it all.

"So?" I gritted my teeth.

"So, what?" he asked.

"Are you going to make a move on her?"

He shrugged. "Why not? You moved on. She's single, and I have always cared about her. I can keep her safe. Clearly you haven't been able to."

I frowned. If he only knew at what lengths I would go—the lengths I did go to try to provide for her. But I didn't have a response because he was right. I had Gabe. By definition, I had moved on and it wasn't fair to Ellie. I couldn't give her a fair answer and had been leading her on the entire time we had been together in the past couple of weeks. I didn't know what to do about her, which shouldn't be Ellie's problem.

Claude went on. "You need to start thinking about what is best for Ellie instead of what is best for you."

With that, he went farther down the trail to pick berries and some of the greens. I felt my face get warm. I was angry he wanted Ellie and approached me like that. Ellie and my woes were none of his business. But I was angrier at myself. I was angry that he had a point—Ellie needed someone better than me. She needed stability and not someone who couldn't deal with his own past.

Claude would be a good man to her—a better man than I could ever be.

He was strong, thoughtful, caring, and he didn't have the blood of thousands on his hands. My breath rate began to increase. I had done so much to hurt these people. Why was I here? Why had I gone along with all this? I couldn't live here. I couldn't face these people.

I glanced over to Claude, who was busy picking berries. I set my basket down and turned the other way and began to walk through the snowy trees and bushes.

I didn't know where I was going, but that didn't matter. If I kept heading down, I would eventually reach the base of these mountains. I just had to get away from them all. I couldn't do this. I wasn't like the others. I couldn't go back to how things were. I couldn't accept the love and care of the people I had hurt so much.

The others didn't understand no matter how hard they tried.

Once I was out of the clearing and away from Claude, I started to quicken my pace. I knew this was a stupid idea and that I would get lost and probably freeze to death, but that didn't matter to me—what mattered was getting away from this guilty feeling I was experiencing.

The world around me felt as if it were spinning. Everything was blurry, and no matter how deep of a breath I took, I was gasping for air. What was wrong with me? What was going on?

Then I heard the sound of gunfire not too far to my right, and quickly after, I felt pain in my leg. I collapsed to the ground.

"Oh shit! Cor!" I heard Ellie's voice in the distance.

I glanced down, the pain bringing my attention

back to the present. My pant leg began to stain red as did the snow I lay on. I stared at it.

Did Ellie just shoot me?

CHAPTER XV

Ellie

"Welp," my brother commented as he lowered his rifle. "You shot Cor. I consider you the victor of this match."

I smacked my brother before I ran to Cor's side. I had shot him in the leg, which was better than many alternatives. I prayed I had only grazed him. I hadn't meant to hit him. I was just trying to scare him and shoot in front of him. He had been so unpredictable in the way he was moving, I shouldn't have done it, but I knew I had to stop him.

Because I could tell he was making a run for it.

It was stupid and petty, but he had a bad habit of running away from his problems, and I didn't want him to do it again—especially since he would die out here in the mountains unprepared as he was. So I thought maybe if I shot the ground in front of him, he would think twice and snap out of whatever daze he was in.

Then I accidentally hit him in the leg.

Was my aim off? Or was I just really mad at him and my deepest desires of wanting to shoot him came out? It didn't matter. I had hurt him, and I felt horrible.

I reached Cor and knelt beside him. "Oh my goddess, Cor. I'm so sorry! I didn't mean to hit you!"

"Yes, you did," he moaned. "And I deserved it."

This made me smile just a little, mainly because he was admitting I was right, and I liked it when he did that. I checked his leg. There was a lot of blood, but it appeared that I had only grazed his leg. I didn't see any evidence of the bullet still being in his leg still. That was a good sign. It would be easy to clean up his wound and would require just a few stitches.

But first we would have to get him back to the camp where the doctor was. I could probably clean and wrap it myself, but since we had access to a doctor now, it would be best if a professional did it.

My brother stepped up next to me and peered down at Cor. "Looks like that hurts, Cor."

Cor glanced up at my brother, and I could tell he was biting back a snarky remark. "Yeah, well, you should teach your sister how to shoot better."

"Actually, I think this proves she's a better shot. I always seemed to miss you when we went hunting growing up."

I didn't know if he meant that. It wouldn't have surprised me. I watched as Cor began to open his mouth, but I was quicker to speak up.

"That is enough, you two. This is serious. We need to get him back to the camp."

I heard footsteps and peered up to find Claude

standing there with two baskets.

"What happened?" he asked. "I heard a gunshot and Ellie yelling for Cor. Then when I turned around, Cor was gone."

Cor answered. "I had to go the bathroom, and then Ellie shot me."

That was a lie if I ever heard one. "I said I was sorry."

"Sorry doesn't make my leg any better."

I wanted to say then he shouldn't have made a run for it, but I didn't want the others to know what had really happened. They would ask why, and I doubted Cor wanted to confess the real reason he was trying to make a break for it.

Because he felt guilty.

That or he was mad because Claude had been flirting with me. It was probably both, if I knew Cor well enough, which I did. I shouldn't have told him that Claude asked me out when we were younger and dating. It probably didn't help the situation—a situation that always made him want to run or get in a fight.

Either way, Cor was trying to get out of here and

I would have some strong words for him later.

"Claude, Edmund, can you help him back to camp? I've already had to carry him on my back once before, and he was quite heavy."

"Hey," Cor protested. "I'm not that heavy."

"You are when you are unconscious."

Edmund squeezed my biceps. "Impressive. Under all those clothes you are quite muscular. You didn't used to be that strong. I used to be able to hold you down and win a fight any day of the week. Now I'm not quite sure I would win."

"Yeah, well, I ain't no princess anymore. I had to hold my own in many fights. Now hurry. I can carry the rest of the stuff."

Edmund handed me his rifle. I unloaded both of ours and slung them over my shoulder. I grabbed the two baskets of berries and greens that Claude and Cor had gathered, along with the bag of birds my brother and I had shot and followed Edmund and Claude as they helped Cor up the mountain.

As I peered at the back of Cor's head, the anger and frustration came boiling to the surface. I wanted to yell at him. I wanted to tell him he was betraying me all over again. I wanted to tell him it was like being stabbed in the heart when he tried to run away like this. It wasn't like when we were kids. Back then it was to get away from the things that were happening around us. Back then I knew where to find him, and I could rely on that. The past three years, however, I didn't know where he was running to, and that scared me. That told me he didn't want me to find him. That he was done with me.

Was he showing me that he was making a decision? Was this him telling me I needed to move on?

I couldn't wait until we could be alone. I was going to give him an earful. Not only was what he was doing hurtful to me, but if he was successful then he would have been leaving Gabe behind as well. What would Gabe have done then? Yes, we had been friends for a couple of weeks now and have risked our lives for each other, but we hadn't known him as long as Cor had. They were way closer than any of us were. He had nowhere else to go. He would be stranded here with people he didn't know.

Then there was the other side of it. I knew it was painful for him to see our people after everything that had happened. When I saw him running down that path, I could tell he couldn't see clearly. He was having a panic attack—a major one. I had experienced one similar when I found out Kaus had been destroyed and I had thought all my family had been destroyed with it. That was why I was trying to shoot near him—I was trying to snap him out of it. I hadn't meant to actually hit him.

But hey, it seemed to have worked. He was more focused now.

At least it had only been a graze. I would have felt horrible if it had been any worse. I had aimed low, so it wasn't as if it would have hit him anywhere vital, but I still shouldn't have done what I did. It wasn't safe, clearly.

It did feel a little satisfying, however. And I could tell my brother was satisfied as well. Although I had a feeling he was joking about trying to shoot him when we were younger, I knew he wanted to deep down. Which was a little scary, to be honest, since my brother wasn't the violent type.

It wasn't as if Cor had done anything specific to make my brother angry with him, it was just something that happened over time. Perhaps it was the skipping school, or getting in trouble on the moon, or when he caught us with our clothes off once in my bedroom. No, I had a feeling it all just added up over time. My brother didn't know what lengths Cor was trying to go to give me a good life. I hadn't even known.

But then it all led to where we were at now.

We made it back to the camp after about an hour or so of walking. We weren't too far, but it was slow going since Cor couldn't put weight on his leg. Claude and Edmund took Cor to the makeshift hospital they had going. It was a larger building compared to the homes in the settlement with several beds and simple medical equipment. There had been no people inside, and after the two of them set Cor on a bed, Claude rushed out.

"I'll go look for the doctor," he called back.

Edmund and I stood by Cor's bed. I grabbed his hand and squeezed it.

"I'm so sorry, Cor. I really am," I said. "I didn't think I would actually hit you."

"It's fine, Ellie. I know you wouldn't mean me any harm. It was just an accident."

That wasn't completely true, but I smiled a little.

"What were you doing so far from Claude?" Edmund asked. "I know where he usually goes to pick berries. It was nowhere near that. That's why we hunt in that area—so we don't have to worry about anyone accidentally shooting someone."

Cor shrugged. "As I said, I had to pee, and I didn't want to pee anywhere near the things we were picking. Then I got a bit turned around."

"Mmm," Edmund commented. He didn't add anything, but I knew he didn't believe Cor's lie. It wasn't that Edmund could tell when Cor was lying but more that he didn't ever believe anything that came out of Cor's mouth.

I shook my head. "It doesn't matter. The important thing is that we're here now and the doctor should be able to fix you up. I mean, even I could fix that wound. It isn't that bad."

Edmund turned to me. "Have you had to fix a lot

of wounds?"

I shrugged. "Yeah. Sure. Zach and I got into a lot of trouble over the years. Although I got shot more than he did. I can be a bit reckless."

"You can say that again," Cor sighed as he leaned his head back.

"But we're safe here," I added for emphasis. Cor turned his attention to me, knowing that I meant he should stop worrying about someone finding out the truth. "We have nothing to worry about here."

Before he could say anything, Claude came back with the doctor. I recognized him from when we were growing up.

"Dr. Pheles. It has been a while." I smiled. "I thought I saw you during the dinners, but we were still keeping to ourselves for the most part."

"It's good to see you are alive and well, Ellie. And Cor, well, it seems you are in trouble again. Things haven't changed, have they?"

"And Ellie was the one that caused it, so things really haven't changed," Cor added.

I stuck my tongue out at him.

Pheles sat down and examined the wound.

"Looks like just a graze. It won't take too long to patch up, but you should keep off of it for the time being."

"That's good," I said.

"You still shot me, Ellie. Don't think because it's a small wound that I'm going to forget."

I frowned. That was fair.

"Now, now. Don't get too upset. You need to rest. Maybe it would be better if all of you left Cor here for the time being," the doctor suggested. "Go get some chores done."

We all nodded, and I knelt beside Cor. "Let's talk later, okay? I'll go let the others know what happened."

He agreed, and I followed my brother and Claude out the door.

CHAPTER XVI

Gabe

It was a lovely day. We'd found somewhere safe in the mountains that was actually rather nice. We had a community where we could trust one another. I smiled as I helped fold the bedding and sheets with Zach since it was laundry day for the community. Nothing could beat this. It was peaceful. No more running. No more people shooting us. No more having to deal with drama. It was all so simple.

I noticed a figure heading toward us, and I glanced up to find it was Ellie. I waved at her.

"Ellie! How was hunting? Did you beat your brother?"

"I shot Cor in the leg. He's going to be fine though."

Okay, maybe it wasn't going to be a nice day.

"What happened?" Zach asked before I could say anything. I couldn't believe what I was hearing. Was it on purpose? Or was it some kind of accident? It had to be an accident, right?

"I… well…" She glanced around. "He can tell you his side of the story, but I sort of was trying to scare him and was aiming for in front of him and missed and hit his leg."

Zach shook his head. "Ellie, what have we talked about regarding gun safety?"

She rolled her eyes. "I know. Don't use a gun to scare people. It only ends up with someone, mainly the other person, getting hurt. Unless I miss, then it ends up with them shooting back at me."

Oh great. This had happened before. That didn't surprise me in the least. Ellie seemed like someone who would shoot to scare people.

"So he is fine? Everything is all right?" I asked.

Ellie nodded. "Yeah, he'll be fine. Might be sore for a while. I only grazed him. Thankfully."

"What did your brother say?" Zach asked.

She let out a sigh. "He said that I won our competition since I shot Cor."

Zach laughed. "Typical. He probably was the one who wanted to do that."

"Yeah, that's pretty much what he said. If my brother saw him, he probably would have shot him first, if I were honest. Maybe."

I still couldn't believe she shot him. What had happened out there? Did they get into a fight? Was he just somewhere he wasn't supposed to be?

"Where is he now?" I asked

Ellie nodded back. "He is getting looked at by a doctor. He should be able to join us tonight. Might need to use crutches for a bit. But otherwise, he will be fine with some rest."

"Should we go check on him? I mean, he got shot…," I asked. I didn't want him to have to be alone at a time like this—not after getting shot. I mean, I would feel a bit lonely and angry if I got injured and no one was there to comfort me.

Ellie shook her head. "No, I think he wants to be alone for a little bit. We can check up on him later. For now, I have been assigned laundry duty with you all."

"That's probably safe," Zach commented. "Can't harm someone doing laundry. At least, I hope you can't. Or else I better worry for my own safety."

Ellie stuck her tongue out at him. She definitely seemed calm about the whole ordeal. If I had shot someone by accident, I didn't know what I would do. I would be panicking. Then again, perhaps she didn't shoot him by accident and there was a reason. They had been fighting for the past couple of days—perhaps she finally let her anger get the better of her.

No, she wouldn't do that. I've seen her mad, but she usually didn't get violent about things—or at least not when it was one of us. She could hold her own in a fight, though, that was for sure. If I had to put money on any of us for a brawl, I would put all my money on Ellie.

Ellie began to help Zach fold laundry. I still wasn't sure what I wanted to do at that moment. Ellie said to leave Cor alone, but I felt almost guilty about it. I didn't know where the hospital area was, however, so it was probably best if I just stayed here.

I went back to folding laundry with the others, but I didn't say much as Ellie and Zach talked about what other things happened that day. Apparently, Ellie was about to shoot a couple of birds before she shot Cor. That wasn't a surprise; she was a great shot.

Except she somehow hit Cor.

He would be fine. I knew that. He had been shot and tortured a few times over the years I had known him. He would survive. This was probably nothing compared to all the times he got beat up. But having someone you cared for and trusted hurt you… that was a different kind of pain. I would know.

I would go check on him after our chores were complete, but by the looks of it, we still had a lot of sheets to wash by hand and let hang dry. I sighed as

I got back to work.

Ellie glanced over to me. "If you really wanted to, you could probably go and check up on him. He's only a few buildings over. I'm sure Zach and I will be able to finish up all this laundry on our own."

I peered over where she said the building was. "Do you think that would be fine? I thought you said the doctor didn't want any visitors."

She shrugged. "He can just send you back here if that is the case. I'm sure Cor wouldn't mind seeing you."

I nodded. "All right. I'll go over and do that. I'll be back later."

Turning toward the building, I headed to where Cor was being treated. As I entered, I saw the doctor stitching up Cor's wound on his leg.

Then everything around me begin to spin and I passed out.

When I awoke, I found myself in a small cot next to Cor. He grinned as he saw my eyes open.

"You okay? You took quite the spill."

The memory came back to me. I had passed out when I saw all the blood on Cor's leg and the needle and thread going into the flesh. I should have been expecting it, but it somehow caught me by surprise. Then I passed out.

"That was embarrassing," I whimpered as I moved. I felt pain in my left shoulder. "Ouch."

"Careful," a man I assumed was the doctor commented. "You sprained your arm when you fell. You will need to rub some ointment on it and use a sling for a couple of days. Otherwise you are fine, at least."

"Thank you very much. I'm truly sorry to add to your workload. I only came here to check on Cor."

"He is doing just fine, so you have nothing to worry about. I have been treating Cor's injuries since he was a small lad, and I can tell you this is one of the least damaging injuries he's had." The old man laughed. "Pardon my rudeness. My name is Malcom Pheles."

"I'm Gabriel Pickett. It's a pleasure."

"So you are the Sirian prince everyone is whispering about. Well, I hope no one has given you any trouble since you have arrived."

"Not at all. Everyone has been friendly."

"That is good. We have been isolated for some time. I always wondered how people would act if an outsider came here. It's good to see the people can still trust after everything."

I didn't know what to say to that. These people had been through a lot, and there was nothing I could do or say that could change that.

"Whelp." The doctor stood up from his chair. "I'll leave you two here to rest for a bit. I'll come back around and check on you, but right now I have some house calls I need to finish."

"Thank you, Doctor," Cor said.

"Yes, thank you!" I called after.

Dr. Pheles waved goodbye, leaving Cor and me alone.

I turned to Cor. "So tell me what happened."

He laughed. "That didn't take long."

"Well, Ellie came over and told Zach and me that she shot you."

"That's it?"

I nodded. He chuckled again. "Typical Ellie."

"So she did shoot you?" I asked.

"Yeah, right in the leg." That was all he said, as if he didn't want to elaborate further.

"Why?" I finally asked.

He let out a sigh. "She… I don't know. I did something stupid, and she called me out on it. It probably didn't help she was already mad at me and everything going on with Claude. She says she wasn't actually aiming for me, but I have a feeling deep down she was. Doesn't matter. It only grazed me. And I probably deserved it."

"Why do you think you deserved it?" I asked. "I mean, weren't you just out there picking berries? What could you have done to make her mad?"

Cor frowned and shook his head. "I got in a fight with Claude although I'm not sure if Ellie knew that. Then I started to wander off, and she saw me going off on my own and was trying to catch my attention."

He was wandering off? That didn't seem right. In fact, it seemed dangerous. "What if you got lost? I would have been worried sick."

"Exactly why Ellie shot me. To stop me from

doing something stupid."

I felt like there was more to the story, but Cor wasn't going to tell me. I reached out to his hand and squeezed it. "Well, I'm glad you're all right. Just promise me you won't go and do something stupid again—otherwise Ellie might shoot your arm or something."

He laughed. "All right. I promise."

CHAPTER XVII

Zach

"So are you going to tell me what really happened?" I asked as we folded some of the sheets that Gabe and I had washed that day. Although there weren't that many people in the settlement, it sure seemed like there was a lot of laundry. Even when it was just Ellie and I, it felt like we always needed to do laundry. I absolutely hated it.

Ellie glanced around. I figured she would tell me

the truth since there weren't any people in our vicinity and Gabe wasn't here. I had a feeling the reason she shot him had to do a little bit about their feelings for one another and she wasn't going to tell Gabe about that.

"What? How Cor was being Cor again? You know how he is. He decided it would be a good idea to try to run away from his problems, and I stopped him before he could get too far."

I let out a breath. I knew it, he did try to make a run for it. "Why didn't you just let him run? That's what he wants."

She grabbed one of the sheets and ruffled with it for a moment, her anger getting the better of her. "Because he would end up getting hurt out there. This isn't exactly the most peaceful area of Mu. He would probably freeze to death. I couldn't live with myself if I let that happen. I would have been worried day and night until we found him again, if we ever did."

I knew she had a point. Cor and I had our differences, but he was still a friend that I would have worried about. It would have been devastating if we found him later frozen to death.

"So the only thing you could think of to stop him was to shoot him?"

"I was angry, okay? I didn't mean to hit him." She sighed. "Maybe I did. I don't know." She finished folding the sheet that was in her hands. "I'm just frustrated about all of this."

"Want to talk about it?" I asked. "I mean, a lot has happened in the past couple of weeks. We have faced a lot on top of all our personal issues we already had going on." The personal issues meaning whatever was going on between her and Cor. Our relationship was fine, and we all got along except when it came to their romantic feelings. It was growing tiresome for me, but that didn't mean I wouldn't be there for my best friend.

"I'd rather deal with people shooting me than the weird love square-triangle thing I have found myself in. I don't know if I should confess my feelings to Cor, or if he would even accept them because of Gabe and all the guilt he has. I don't know, maybe I should just accept Claude's proposal."

I frowned. "I thought you didn't have feelings for Claude."

She shrugged. "I don't hate him. I love Cor, but I just can't deal with all the shit that comes with that. Then there's Gabe. I don't want him to get hurt. Claude would always be there for me and wouldn't run away like Cor has again and again. I could love something stable like that."

I wrapped my arms around her. "I don't know how to help you other than be here for you. You know I don't feel like that for anyone, so I can't give you that great of advice. But I do know that I'll always be here for you as a friend or like a brother. I'll never run away, and I'll happily stay by your side until the end of time."

She squeezed me back. "Thank you, Zach. I needed to hear that. You are the bestest friend someone like me could ever wish for. I would never leave you either."

I knew she meant that, but something in the back of my mind always worried she would run away with Cor and leave me behind. Besides her, I didn't have anyone growing up. The thought haunted my nightmares.

What if they all left me and I found myself truly alone?

To find out that Cor had been studying to go to a university brought up the feeling that they would have left me all over again. Did he plan to bring me along with Ellie, or was he just going to leave me behind in Kaus as they made their new life together in some foreign zone? Life didn't end up that way, and it was actually Cor who ended up being alone, but that didn't mean the fear wasn't there.

Ellie always said she would never leave me behind, but it was what my father said before he abandoned my mother and me. My mother was never the same after he left. It was about the time I started getting bullied about being half-human. People of all ages were relentless. Except for Cor and Ellie. They stood up for me and made it all stop. But I heard the whispers. No one wanted anything to do with me. If they left me, I would have no one then and I would have no one now.

Which was why I was leery about being here.

Sure, we were currently safer. However, I

couldn't believe all the prejudices they had against half Kausians would simply go away—not after what happened. But they welcomed us with open arms. No one had said anything about me or about Gabe.

What was going on?

Were they planning something? If they were, today would have been the perfect day to corner Gabe and I as Ellie and Cor had gone out to forage and hunt. The four people that would have protected us were gone. Was it because Mae said we were to be trusted and accepted? Did they have that much confidence in her and in the council? Or was something else going on?

"Should we finish this laundry?" Ellie asked as she let go of me.

I had completely forgotten what we were doing. Ellie was still in my arms, and I had completely lost my mind for a moment. I quickly nodded. "Yeah, let's."

She eyed me. "Is something wrong?"

I shook my head. "No. I'm just still in shock that you shot Cor."

Ellie examined me a moment longer and frowned. "You know if something is on your mind, you can talk to me. I have your back as much as you have mine."

I gave her my most sincere smile. "I know, Ellie. It's nothing. We've just been through a lot in the past couple of weeks. I am not used to staying still like this. Everything is just sort of seeping in, you know? We were almost killed multiple times. We are wanted for goddess knows what now in the nations…it's just strange to finally be somewhere where we don't have to worry about what we need to eat, where to sleep, and if we need to sneak out in the middle of the night. We finally found a home and it just seems too good to be true."

She nodded. "Yeah, I know what you mean. It all feels unreal. But if there is anything else, just talk to me, okay? I know I'm not the only one who has baggage."

"You can say that again." I let out a breath. "But these sheets aren't going to dry themselves.

She turned to the next load we needed to dry and sighed. "Well, let's get at it."

* * *

It seemed like the laundry would never end, but we finally took down the last sheet that had dried, and I felt as if I were ready to collapse. I hoped we wouldn't have to do that every day. According to Mae, everyone cycles through chores. I was curious what we would be doing tomorrow.

As we headed toward the community area for dinner, we spotted Cor and Gabe walking there as well. Cor was on crutches, as I expected, but Gabe's arm was in a sling.

I pointed at Gabe. "What happened to you?"

His face turned red. "I don't want to talk about it. It was really stupid."

Cor grinned. "He passed out when he saw the doctor sewing up my leg."

"Oh no! That's terrible! Are you okay?" I asked.

"It was just a sprain. It will heal up soon," Gabe explained. "It was really stupid."

Cor sighed. "And I'm going to be fine, thank you for asking."

I turned to him. "I already knew you were going to be fine. Ellie said she only grazed you."

Cor rolled his eyes. "Only grazed me. She could have taken my foot off."

"I said I was sorry," Ellie interjected as she crossed her arms. "We all know it was your fault anyway."

The two of them glared at each other, then both turned toward where food was being served. Gabe and I shrugged at each other. He clearly didn't know what was going on, and I wasn't going to explain. It wasn't my place. Besides, Cor would be mad if he actually had to tell someone his feelings. And I doubted he wanted Gabe to know he would have left him behind here with a bunch of people he didn't know all that well.

Supper was the same as the night before, but I wasn't complaining. I loved all the food we had. I took a seat next to Ellie, and Cor and Gabe took a seat across from us.

As we ate, I swore I heard someone whispering across the area from us. I glanced up and saw they were looking at us. Were the whispers about me? Were they finally showing their true colors? Were they talking about my red hair? Were they talking about how I wasn't a true Kausian because my father was a human? Were they saying how I should have never been born?

The world around me felt as if it were closing in. Were these people going to turn on me? Was this welcoming behavior just a ruse? Were they going to leave me out in the mountain with no supplies and laugh as I froze to death?

My thoughts were interrupted when two female Kausians came to our table both with long white hair. "May we sit here?"

The four of us scooted over so they could join us. We weren't going to decline such a request since we were the guests to this settlement. At least, until we felt truly accepted.

"My name is Velma, and this here is Roxie. We just wanted to welcome you personally to our community. It has been quite a while since any outsiders have stumbled upon our people."

"I mean," Cor began, "we aren't exactly outsiders. We're from Kaus."

Velma nodded as she glanced around. "Right. I more mean our community since moving to the mountains. We all, of course, grew up in Kaus, which is usually the only reason Mae allows outsiders in."

"So other Kausians have found this place?" Ellie asked as she took a bite of her deer meat. "We were led to believe no one has found this place."

Roxie answered, "Yes. They didn't stumble by accident like we heard you did, but every once in a while a scouting party will go down and find some Kausians and get any supplies we might need. It's a dangerous mission, as our location can't be discovered, but we have a group that is willing to risk their life to find more of our kind."

This was news to us. We were told they didn't venture out of the settlement in fears of getting found out. Perhaps we were told that so we didn't wander off. We weren't yet trusted. "Oh? Where are these scouts now?" I asked.

"They are looking for people right now, actually. They should be back soon," Roxie answered.

Cor appeared as if he had seen a ghost. I wondered why that was. Did he think it was possible someone on the outside would know that he was to blame for the codes leaking? If these people didn't know yet, and they had already found outsiders, the odds were slim.

"We haven't let in any half-Kausians though. Or people from other races," Velma commented as she glanced to Gabe and me.

My heart felt as if it were being squeezed. "That's because there aren't many of us out there." I picked at my food with my fork. I didn't like where this was going.

"Well, you are welcome here either way. We just want to survive." Velma gave me a smile.

I peered down at my food. Was I welcomed here? I would more than likely be the only half-Kausian. I didn't know how many of them survived after the attack, not to mention there weren't many of us to begin with. We stood out like a sore thumb with our red hair, which caused us to be singled out whenever possible.

Standing up, I excused myself. "I'm not very hungry and am kind of tired. Please excuse me for the night."

With that, I left the table. I swore I heard

whispers about me as I passed each table, but perhaps I was wrong. Perhaps they weren't there, and it was all in my head. Perhaps the whispers I heard were just ghosts of the past.

What was I going to do to make them shut up?

CHAPTER XVIII

Cor

The leg wound still hurt a lot.

I didn't want to grumble about it—it was just a flesh wound. I had worse done to me many times, but for some reason this one really stung. Was it because Ellie was the one who shot me? I wasn't sure. All I knew was that I was pissed. I was pissed at her. I was pissed at Claude for taking a seat next to her once Zach got up. I was pissed I had to witness his endless flirting.

And I was pissed with myself for not making up my own damn mind.

It shouldn't be this hard, yet I couldn't bring myself to tell her and Gabe how I felt. Would there be a way I could just be with both of them? Would that be fair to either of them?

I finished my food as Ellie, Gabe, Edmund, and Claude all talked among themselves. I knew Gabe had noticed my quietness, but he didn't say anything. I had a feeling Ellie had as well, but she was still mad at me and flirting back to Claude. I couldn't blame her for being mad at me, though.

I had tried to make a run for it.

But I couldn't help it—not after everything. She didn't understand the pain and guilt that I felt when I saw all these people. It was my fault they were out here. It was my fault that they all lost so many loved ones.

And she didn't know the real truth.

She didn't know that I had worked for Krax and had assassinated some of our kind for him in order to get closer to him. I wanted to kill Krax myself, and I had used any means to try to achieve that goal. Then I didn't even get to kill him. Byron did. Then I didn't even get to kill Byron. Jonathan did. It was just one bad guy after another.

So what was the point of it all?

I had done horrible things and had nothing to show for it. All of what transpired would have happened if I hadn't been an assassin for Krax. I had made a huge mistake, and I couldn't do anything to make it right again. I would always have to live with this guilt.

After finishing my plate of food, I stood up. "I'm going to go rest. I got shot and all that."

Gabe was quick to stand. "Do you need help?"

I shook my head. "No, stay here and have fun. I don't need any help."

He gave me a once-over, then nodded. I honestly wanted to be alone. It wasn't that I didn't want him near, I just needed a moment to myself—a moment to take in everything.

I was about halfway back to the hut we had created when I heard steps behind me. I stopped and turned to find Ellie there, her arms folded against her chest, frowning.

We both stood there for an awkward moment when I finally commented, "Did you want something?"

"I… I just want to say I'm sorry. I shouldn't have shot you. It was out of line."

I was surprised. Ellie never had apologized for hurting me in the past. She usually said I deserved it. "Thanks."

"I should have just ran to you and punched you in the jaw instead. It would have been a lot more satisfying."

I rolled my eyes but smiled a little. She definitely meant it. I missed her frankness. "Well, good to know. If I see you barreling toward me, I will run for my life."

"I'd like to see you try," she said, jesting. I saw her lip twitch as if she wanted to smile.

We stood there for another quiet moment. Why was this so awkward? We had known each other almost our entire lives. We knew everything about each other.

No, that wasn't true. I didn't know what she went

through for the past three years, and she didn't know what I had done to try to take Krax down in the past three years. I had done everything to get close to him, including betraying our own kind.

We were practically strangers at this point trying to act like these three years haven't happened and we can go back to what our lives were like before.

"Are we going to talk about the fact that you tried to run away?" she whispered. "Or are you just going to ignore it like you do all your problems?"

I frowned. "It's not easy to talk about. You wouldn't understand."

"Oh yeah? Try me."

I glanced around. If I did tell her the truth, I definitely didn't want anyone listening in. "You aren't going to let this go, are you?"

"Have you ever known me to let anything go?"

I let out a breath. She had a point there. "Fine. Let's go back to the house thing. I don't want to talk out here."

She followed me back to Gabe and my new home. She opened the door for me since my hands were occupied with the crutch and helped me inside. I sat down on the ground where there were sleeping bags, and she sat across from me, waiting.

I let out a sigh. "It's just really hard to be here, Ellie. I don't know what to do."

"Because of what happened three years ago?"

I nodded and looked down at my lap. "It's all my fault. I shouldn't have trusted him. All of this wouldn't have happened if I were just smarter."

"It's not your fault, Cor. Look at me."

I glanced up. She was as serious as she always was.

"This is not your fault. You were used and tricked and beaten. You had no choice. If it wasn't you, it would have been some other way."

"But it was me. You don't get it. I should have sacrificed my life to keep Kaus safe. But I didn't and then look at what happened."

"You didn't know the extent of their plan. If you didn't tell them, they would have killed you and then found another way in. You know that."

I shook my head. "Ellie, you don't know that."

She placed her hand on my leg. "Yes, I do. We have seen the lengths in which Byron would have gone. He was a monster, and so is his brother. We stood no chance. So please stop thinking about it. None of this was your fault."

I looked back down at the ground. Even if I could stop feeling guilty about it all, that didn't matter. I still had done horrible things for Krax, trying to get close to him.

"What is it?"

I shook my head. "You would never forgive me if you knew the truth, Ellie. I just… I can't be here."

She was quiet for a moment and then moved over next to me. She grabbed my hand and squeezed it. "Is this about what you did for Krax?"

I turned to her, surprised. How did she…? Then I remembered. She had found the files on her and Zach. She knew I had been a bounty hunter. I looked back down at the ground.

"I have done horrible, horrible things. I should have just given up. I should have found you and we should have figured it out years ago."

"You had no choice. I had no choice but to become a bounty hunter as well. Zach and I have done things we don't want to think about either just to survive. I don't know how many of those people were innocent. I have started more fights than you can imagine. You aren't the only one who has baggage, Cor. It's fine."

"But did you hunt your own people down, Ellie? Did you kill Kausians to get closer to someone who wasn't even the person you should have been targeting? Did you figure a couple of lives were worth the revenge you sought? Only to find out it was all for nothing? You didn't have to kill those people. You didn't have to kill family members or friends of the people here. You don't have to wonder if they would have found this place and would have been reunited if it weren't for you."

Ellie was silent. She knew I was right. I was a monster. I had no redemption. I had no way to clean the blood off my hands. I didn't deserve to be welcomed by her like she and the others did. Worst of all, I didn't deserve to be with her, and I knew it.

I shook my head. "Just let me go, Ellie. Live a happy life here with Claude. Enjoy the life you deserve. Forget about me."

Ellie kicked me in the leg where the wound was.

I let out a little scream.

"You bitch, that hurt!"

"Well, it seems like pain is the only way I can get you to come to the present. You keep letting yourself get trapped in your mind and don't let others in, or at least you don't let other people's opinions into your brain."

"You think if we told everyone what happened that they would have the same opinion as you? Or would they just want me dead?"

"I know you better than they do, Cor."

"Do you?" I asked.

She was silent. Eventually she let go of my hand and stood up. "Cor, I'm only going to say this once, so listen to me closely. If you keep pushing people away and running from your problems, you are going to find that one of these times you are going to push people too far and no one is going to come help you. You'll be all alone. Do you really want that?"

With that, she turned and left me sitting there. I leaned back on the bed and took a deep breath. I pulled out the engagement ring that was still in my pocket, as it always had been. She was right. She was always right.

The problem was that I did feel as if I deserved to be all alone.

CHAPTER XIX

Ellie

Well, that went as well as expected.

I let out a sigh as I headed back to where everyone was finishing their dinner and singing and dancing. Cor had always internalized everything. I knew that. But he needed to either face his problems or leave us all behind. It wasn't fair for me, and it wasn't fair to Gabe.

As I began to head back, I decided to check in

with Zach. It wasn't like him to abandon food at the table. He never wasted food, nor had I ever heard him say he wasn't that hungry. There was something wrong—that was clear when we were talking earlier.

And those two women mentioning how they didn't let half-Kausians in probably didn't help.

I knocked on the door before opening it. "Hey, Zach, are you okay?" I asked.

He was laying on his sleeping bag, staring up at the ceiling. As he glanced over to me, I noticed his eyes were red. He quickly wiped away the tears.

"Ellie, you're back so soon?"

"Not exactly—I decided to come and check on you." I decided not to mention I had followed Cor back. It would have sounded as if I hadn't cared. "What's wrong?"

He shook his head. "It's nothing. Don't worry about it."

I plopped down next to him. "It's not nothing. I know my best friend well enough to know something is up. Now spill the beans."

Zach turned to me. "I just…it's a lot being here,

Ellie."

Was that this group's motto? "What do you mean?"

I knew Cor had his reasons for feeling out of place here, but I wasn't sure what Zach was referring to.

"I just… it's hard to believe that they all have changed. That they all now accept me. I mean, Mae was always helpful when we lived in Kaus, but what about all these other people? They wouldn't give me the time of day in Kaus and now they want to be my friend and help me move in and all that. It's just… I don't know."

I wrapped my arms around Zach as he cried. "It's okay. You have every right to be upset with them even though now they are acting accepting. It's up to you to forgive them, but whatever you choose you need to decide for yourself."

"It's not whether or not I forgive them, it's whether or not I can trust them. I feel as if every whisper is about me and that they are planning something against Gabe and I."

"Listen to me. If any of these people lay a finger

on you, I will destroy them with my own bare hands. You got that? You have nothing to worry about with me here."

"I know you are there for me, but it doesn't mean it doesn't hurt, Ellie. I just… I need some time to clear my head and accept where we are and everything that happened when we were younger."

My heart ached for Zach. He didn't deserve having to feel like this. He was the bestest of friend one could ask for and just a big ball of sunshine. Back then people judged him because of heritage, and it just wasn't fair.

"Do you mind just leaving me alone? Go back to Claude and the others," he said.

"Are you sure? I can stay here with you if you want me to."

He shook his head. "No, I want to be alone. Go be with the others."

I kissed his cheek. "If you insist. But you know where to find me if you need me."

He nodded. "I know."

I got up and left him there. I didn't want to, but if it was what he wanted, I would do as he asked. I wiped away a tear as I stepped out of our little home to find Claude waiting for me. I didn't feel like dealing with him after everything, but he didn't deserve the emotional turmoil I had due to both Cor and Zach. I took a deep breath and tried to calm myself down.

"Oh hey, Claude. Do you need something?" I asked with a smile.

"I just wanted to check on you to make sure you are fine."

I glanced back at both Cor's and my own hut. "I'm fine. Can't say the same for Cor. He has that gunshot and all."

"Were you two just talking? In your home?"

I shook my head. "No, we talked in his hut and then I went to check on Zach. I just wanted to apologize to Cor. I was the one who shot him."

"Yeah. I still can't believe all that happened. What was going on? How did you accidentally hit him?" Claude asked.

"I… I was trying to hit the ground in front of him, but he moved too fast. I shouldn't have done it. It was wrong."

"I still don't know what he was doing all the way out there. I mean, I turned for a moment and he was long gone. If he was just using the bathroom, he should have been closer. He knew you all were hunting in that area."

I didn't like where that was going. Did he know something about Cor? "He gets turned around a lot."

"Do you think he was trying to run away?"

Whelp. He came out and said it. I shrugged. "I don't know. I wouldn't see why he would do such a thing." That was a lie, but I couldn't let Claude know what was troubling Cor. The two of them never did get along.

"I hope it wasn't because I talked to him before that moment…" Claude scratched the back of his head. "I would feel rather guilty if it were."

That was the first time I was hearing about it. "What did you two talk about?"

"I may have told him he shouldn't string you along like he was. I mean, he brought his boyfriend here and expects you to still be there for him?"

I shook my head. "It isn't that simple, Claude.

Please just mind your own business."

He stepped forward and stroked my cheek with his thumb. "I can't just stand by and watch someone I love get taken advantage of. You deserve better than that."

I stared into his golden eyes. Had they always sparkled as much as they had? I almost felt as if he had a point. I did deserve someone who would be there for me.

"It's not that simple, Claude. He and I had loved each other for many years."

"And yet he found someone else while you were separated."

We were both quiet. He did find someone else, but I knew he was partially using Gabe or at least at the time. Then he grew to love Gabe, which I couldn't blame him. Gabe was a nice guy.

Claude leaned in closer and kissed me on the lips. I didn't push him away. I didn't exactly pull him closer either. I didn't know what I wanted to do. I wanted things to be simple. Staying with Claude would be simple. But was that what I really wanted?

He backed away and leaned his forehead on my own. "Will you at least give me a chance? After all this time?"

I slowly nodded. "Fine. But you get to tell my brother. He's going to be mad at you."

He smiled. "That seems like a good deal to me. And your brother wouldn't mind me taking you away from Cor."

That was fair. He really did hate Cor.

"But this will be a trial thing. I can't promise you that I'll love you the way I loved Cor."

He smiled a little. "See right there? You are already speaking in past tense."

He was right. I said that I had loved him. Is he right? Am I already moving on?

I still loved Cor—I knew that. But was it the same feeling I had when we were just silly teenagers? Or had everything that had happened temper that feeling? Or was it the fact that he had moved on and my heart had decided perhaps I should do the same?

Claude grabbed my hand and led us back to the community area. I couldn't look my brother in the eye when we arrived at the table, as I could feel them on our connected hands.

"About time," my brother murmured. "I thought you were going to melt the moment you saw her."

I blushed. Although I knew Claude had always had feelings for me, but the fact he had held on to them all this time was jarring. Perhaps I could grow to have the same feelings for him, if he had been willing to wait all this time.

Because Cor clearly hadn't.

But he had our engagement ring on him, as I still had mine. It was still around my neck. After all this time.

Did true love exist? Or did love come and go like the waves on a beach?

"Is Cor okay?" Gabe asked. I had completely forgotten he was there. Now I felt even more embarrassed because he knew the whole story. Well, most of it.

"Yeah. He's fine," I answered.

I knew he meant about Claude and not the wound. Cor didn't know yet, and I didn't want to be there when he found out. He was going to be upset. But he had his chance. He knew what he was doing was pushing me away, and he did nothing to stop it.

After the initial awkwardness wore off, we talked about all sorts of things from how this camp got started to the different types of plants one would find in the area. Claude took me to dance by the music, and after a couple of hours, people started to retire for the night.

Claude walked me back to my hut. I felt embarrassed even though it was pretty close to his own. We stood in front of the door, quiet. I rocked on my heels, not sure what to do next. It had been so long since I dated someone.

"Well, good night. I'll see you tomorrow, yeah?" Claude asked.

I nodded. "I believe I'm not allowed to hunt for a while. But I should see you around. I think I have kitchen duty tomorrow."

"Well, I look forward to eating your cooking." He leaned in and kissed me on the lips. It was a soft, gentle kiss. He backed away and smiled.

"Yeah, well." I took a breath to calm my racing

heart. "You may regret that comment tomorrow."

He laughed as he turned to leave. "We shall see."

I watched him walk away for a moment and then turned to Zach's and my hut. Zach was already in bed.

"You still awake?" I whispered.

He didn't respond. I wasn't sure if he was faking because he didn't want to talk about earlier, but I didn't push to find out. I wanted to tell him about Claude to see what he thought about this mess, but he had his own shit to deal with. I let out a sigh.

It wasn't that I didn't care for Claude. I just didn't feel that fiery passion like I had with Cor when we were younger. Was that because I was younger, and love was new? Had I grown up and this is what love was supposed to feel like? Or was I lying to myself?

There was only one way to find out.

CHAPTER XX

Gabe

A lot happened yesterday, and as I woke up, all the memories slowly came back to me. I stretched, and that was when the memory of hurting my shoulder came back to me. I grimaced in pain. That was right. I had hurt it when I went to visit Cor in the infirmary. He was in the infirmary because Ellie shot him. Ellie and he also had some kind of fight, which more than likely had to do with her getting together with Claude, who was Ellie's brother's best friend.

All of it made my brain hurt more than my arm.

I presumed Cor and Ellie were still fighting since when I got back to the hut, Cor was moping and acting like he was asleep. I could tell he wasn't actually asleep, but I didn't say anything. I didn't want to get in the middle of it all, not to mention Cor rarely opened up about things like that. I couldn't blame him; he had been through a lot.

It wasn't as if I opened up to him that often in the past two years either. No, both of us carried secrets of our past that we didn't want to face. Both of us had baggage, which is why we could understand each other. It always felt like us against the world. In the beginning I hadn't known it was quite literally.

Then there was Zach. I wasn't sure what happened during dinner, but he appeared rather flustered, almost as if he had seen a ghost. Maybe he had known the people they were talking to, or perhaps he remembered something. Or perhaps he realized who hadn't survived the attack.

Although it was surprising how many people survived the attack on Kaus, I knew there had to be a lot of people missing. People at the center of the attack would have been killed. I presumed all their families had been killed besides Ellie's brother. I knew what losing family felt like but not at the quantity that all these people dealt with.

My mother's death still haunted my nightmares. I should have known that Byron was going to kill her. I should have kept her safe. But instead, I had done nothing. I assumed Byron was only after me, but he had an entire plot put together. Now the events played over and over again every time I slept, and I would have to live with the burden for the rest of my life.

Was this how Cor felt? Was this why it was so hard for him to move on?

I glanced over to Cor to find him still sound asleep. I had a feeling we would need to wake soon to find out what our chores would be for the day. I poked his arm, and his eyes flickered open. He smiled when he saw my face, which made my insides get all warm and fuzzy.

"Morning beautiful." Cor smiled. "Did you sleep well?"

I didn't, but I wasn't going to tell him that. "I did. How about you?"

"I slept fine."

Did we always start our mornings with lies? I began to wonder since now I knew the truth about his past. I leaned forward and gave him a kiss.

"Ready to see what they have planned for us today?" I asked.

He sighed. "Not really, but I can't imagine it can be any worse than hunting with Ellie."

I was glad he could stay humorous through everything that had happened. He still didn't know about Claude and Ellie though. Or at least I didn't think he did.

I was surprised when she came back with Claude holding his hand. I could tell she was still battling with what she felt on the inside and not sure if it was the right path for her, but to be honest, it gave me a sense of relief. Then perhaps Cor would stop pursing Ellie and would commit his heart to me. Was that selfish? Perhaps so, but I couldn't help it. I didn't know what I would do without him.

We got up and helped each other get dressed as we were both wounded from the day before. My shoulder felt a little better, but I kept using the sling as I didn't want to make it worse.

"Did you have fun last night with the others?" Cor asked as he fixed his collar.

"Um, yeah. I did. Got to hear some stories about Ellie and her brother. They are quite the siblings."

"Ellie has definitely always looked up to her brother. I'm glad that didn't stop her from dating me though. But she tries to outdo him in everything. It usually ends up with them getting into some kind of trouble, though."

"Yeah, it seems like it." I was quiet for a moment.

Cor didn't seem like he was mad at her, so perhaps she didn't tell him she was dating Claude. I debated on telling him. Should I? Or should I keep quiet about it? Did it matter? The two of us were a couple—it shouldn't have mattered if Ellie were seeing someone else. That is, unless Cor was fixating for the right opportunity to dump me and get back with her. Was he going to do that? Would her running off with someone else push him to finally make that decision? Or would it make him just settle for me?

"What's wrong?" Cor asked.

I must have been obvious about worrying about everything. I took a deep breath. "Um, what did you and Ellie talk about last night?"

He furrowed his eyebrows. "Why, what did she say?"

"Um, well…" There was no point in lying about it now. "She and Claude…"

He frowned. "Did they become a couple?"

I nodded slowly. Cor finished fixing his collar and shrugged. "Doesn't matter to me. We aren't a couple. Not anymore."

That was a lie if I ever did hear one. "If you want to talk about it…"

"Nope. There is nothing to talk about. She is free to choose who she wants. Claude is a good guy, and she deserves someone who can be there for her and make her happy."

While I knew he did feel she deserved someone

to make her happy, I didn't quite buy all that. "Okay. If you say so."

He turned to me and smiled. "Now let's go see what we're supposed to be doing today."

I had hoped he would say it didn't matter because he was with me, but he never said those words, which meant it really did bother him. Did he want to be with Ellie more than he wanted to be with me? I knew they were childhood sweethearts, so did that mean I never stood a chance? Was I just second place to him? Was I just to fill in the loneliness he had when he was with her?

Not wanting to deal with these feelings, I followed Cor out the door, helping him as he was still on crutches. We made our way to the town center where the job list was posted for the day. We searched for our names.

"Looks like we have watch duty since we can't move that well. Perfect," Cor commented as his eyes lingered on the paper. I could tell he was checking for the others.

"Zach and Ellie have kitchen duty, and Claude and Edmund have cleaning duty."

He turned to me. "I wasn't checking for them."

"Why not? They're our friends. I checked as well." I knew it was because he didn't want to see if Ellie and Claude were working together today, nor did he want to admit that. He was such an open book.

Cor appeared frustrated and let out a long breath. "Whatever, let's get going."

After breakfast, we made our way to the front of the camp where we would be helping with the lookout. I assumed it wouldn't be that hard of a job since not many seemed to come across the camp, but I knew only a moment could cause all that to change. Who knew at what lengths my father would go if he wanted us captured?

Would he search the mountains though? Or would he presume we would all die out here? There was no way he knew about this colony, otherwise he would have sent people out here to snuff it out.

Unless he really wanted to make sure I was dead.

Was I putting all these people at risk? Or was it the safest place for me to be? I didn't know the answer to that, but I did know that if my father found this place, I would risk my life to keep these people safe.

There were three other lookouts, which seemed to be more than necessary, but I assumed they were overcautious for a reason. They had lost their home before after all.

We took a seat and grabbed some binoculars. There was snow as far as the eyes could see. No surprise there.

"Now we will go over a few things since you two are new. As you can imagine, we don't have many threats out here besides the cold, never-ending snow," a woman with long white hair explained. I believed her name was Rosa. "Sometimes there are creatures that might appear, but they are easy to scare off. But our job is important in case there is a threat, and the other nations find out we survived. We alert the others of an attack, and we're the first line of defense. That cabinet over there is full of guns that we clean and check regularly."

She nodded over to the cabinet. I was surprised they would have so much ammunition.

"Generally, what happens is we get to hang out

all day. It's boring, but we figured due to your injuries, this would be the best job for you two to have for a while. Cor, you can still hold a gun, and your friend, well, he has eyes."

Cor chuckled. "He isn't that good with a gun even when he can use both his arms."

I frowned, but I knew he had a point. "It's true."

"Well, that's okay. You'll learn eventually. Now, do you have any questions?"

Cor and I glanced at each other, then shook our heads.

"Good. Now, who wants to hear the latest gossip?" she asked with a grin.

Cor leaned forward and smiled. "Now this is the Kaus I remember."

CHAPTER XXI

Zach

Had I overreacted last night? I felt like I had. I felt shameful for letting the past affect the happiness I should have felt for finding our people. I should have been happy they all were alive, but instead I worried about myself and was brining everyone else down.

I knew if I told Ellie how I felt, she would smack me and say I shouldn't feel ashamed for how I acted. She knew what I had dealt with as a child, but that was so many years ago. People changed, as we all have clearly seen. I wasn't the same man I was back then—not after everything that had happened. Neither was Ellie and neither was Cor. If we changed as much as we did, I was sure these people had as well.

"Looks like we have kitchen duty," Ellie commented as she searched the schedule.

I glanced at it. "Cor and Gabe have guard duty."

She turned to me. "I wasn't looking for them."

I held up my hands. "It was just a statement."

"Whatever. Let's get to it."

I followed Ellie toward the main kitchen area where food was prepped. We would be prepping lunch and dinner, then tomorrow's breakfast to be ready in the morning. I was glad we didn't have to get up early for today's breakfast prep. I hated mornings.

As we made our way through the maze that was this settlement, we ran into Claude and Edmund. I glanced over to Ellie who was blushing. Perhaps she did have feelings for Claude and just wasn't sure what to do. She had only loved one boy before now—perhaps it was just a matter of her thinking she could only love Cor and she shoved any other thoughts out of her mind. Now that she was free of those ideas, she realized she could love Claude as well.

At least, I hoped that was what was going on. The two of them were cute together and I knew he wouldn't betray her like Cor always seemed to do. If Claude loved her after all this time, then I felt he was a keeper. But if I knew one thing about Ellie and Cor, they couldn't do easy.

I just prayed to the goddess that this didn't blow up in everyone's faces. Was a simple life that hard to ask for?

Edmund stepped up to me as Claude and Ellie talked. "Thank you, by the way."

I glanced over to him with an eyebrow raised. "For what?"

"For keeping Ellie safe all this time."

I laughed. "It's more like she kept me safe. She is way stronger than I am."

"Even so, I think having you around kept her

going. I know if I were alone after everything, I wouldn't have been able to keep going. I assume it took both of you some time to move on with your lives. I am just saying I am glad you were there for her, and that she was there for you."

I stared down at the ground. He had a point—if either of us ended up alone after what had happened, I doubted either of us would have made it far. The world was cruel but together we were able to stay safe, or at least as safe as we were about to be.

"It took some time, to be honest. We thought you were all dead. I am thankful we found this place. I just wish we could have found it sooner."

Edmund nodded. "As do I. I thought my sister was dead. I thought you and Cor were dead. You don't realize what you have until it's gone."

"You can say that again."

"I'm sorry your mother didn't make it," Edmund said.

I let out a breath. "Even if she did, I doubted she would have been able to live out here. She was sick."

"Doesn't make it better, though. So many people were lost that day and we try to honor them as best we can by living another day." Edmund took a deep breath. "Well, we should get to our chores. Claude and I have cleaning duty for the streets and communal areas. We will see you tonight at dinner." He turned to Claude. "Claude, come on! Stop flirting with my sister and get to work."

Ellie stuck her tongue at her brother, but her face was as red as a beet. As the two others walked off, we made our way to the kitchen.

"So, what did the two of you talk about?" I asked.

She shrugged. "Just making plans for later. What about you and my brother?"

"Oh, nothing really. Just small talk."

I didn't want to tell her exactly what he said. It wasn't that I didn't want her to know but it was just a lot to deal with in the morning when we needed to get to work.

There were a couple of others in the kitchen who were there to show us the ropes and help us out since it was our first time. Typically only three people were needed for this job, but since we were new, they assigned a total of four people. Ellie and I knew how to make our own meals, so it wasn't too hard to get a hang of what we needed to do.

"If I ever head out the door of the kitchen," I whispered to Ellie. "I am probably going to the bathroom so don't try to throw a knife at me. I ain't going to try to run away."

"Har, har," Ellie commented. "You are so funny, Zach."

I grinned because it was true—I was funny.

We prepared lunch and I brought out some of the food to the common area as Ellie plated the next side dish. As I walked out, I felt the same aura I had felt the night before—as if someone was judging me. I heard the whispers again.

I hurried back to the kitchen as the other two Kausians took out the remaining food for lunch. I let out a sigh, glad I didn't have to go back out there.

Was it in my head? Or had people actually been talking behind my back?

A couple of more hours passed, and I chopped up

the vegetables for the stew that would be served at dinner that night. Ellie was next to me, washing the potatoes and other root vegetables. She didn't seem to notice my worries after I served the lunch, which I was thankful for. I didn't want to bring them up here.

What if I was imagining it all? What if there were no whispers? What if no one had actually said those things when I was a child? What if it had been all in my head and I simply thought they had been talking about me? What if I had misunderstood?

Had I been I wrong about my own people? Had I thought them to be monsters to me when really I was the monster? Had I turned away people who wanted to be my friend because I thought they meant me harm?

No, that couldn't be the case. I had heard the words myself. People used to corner me and make fun of me. I was there. I had seen it happen.

Then why was everyone so nice to me now?

"Is everything fine?" Ellie asked as she glanced over to me. "You really seemed focused on cutting those roots."

I blinked and glanced over to her. "Huh? Oh, it's nothing."

"That's not nothing. You were upset last night too. Are you still worried?" she asked.

I glanced around. The other Kausians were out of earshot. I sighed as I whispered to her. "It's just that… when we grew up in Kaus, so many people picked on me. Now they are embracing me with open arms, which I'm glad. But it almost feels as if all the things that happened were in my head. That maybe I misunderstood. I don't know, it's just making me feel awful when I know I should feel happy."

Ellie dropped the vegetables she was cleaning and put both her hands on either side of my head. "Now you listen to me right now, Zachariah Richards. It is not your fault what happened in the past. I was there. People did pick on you. As to why they aren't now, I don't know. But that doesn't mean you have to forgive or forget. What you need to do is accept that you are the most beautiful person I know inside and out, and your parents' species does not define who you are as a person. You are my best friend, and I wouldn't have it any other way."

I smiled a little, which sort of hurt as her hands were crushing my cheeks. "Fank fou for dat."

She grinned. "My pleasure." She let go of my cheeks. "But if people do start saying something, they will have me to answer to, you got that? You come straight to me, and I'll scare them off."

"What, are you going to shoot them too?" I jested.

"Maybe. I can't make any promises. But they definitely won't be picking on you again."

"Perhaps that is why no one has said anything yet. They remember you."

"Damn straight they do. I do not mess around." She picked up the knife to cut the vegetables and grinned. "And I'm quite proficient in weapon handling."

"It's a surprise you haven't scared Claude off yet. All the other boys, other than Cor, were quite afraid of you when we were growing up."

She hesitated a moment, then turned to the sink.

"That's because he was my brother's friend. My brother is quite the character as well."

"Yeah, but you are like ten times worse. Admit it, Claude has always had a thing for you, even when you were bouncing off the walls and getting in all sorts of trouble."

Ellie smiled gently for a moment. "I guess he has. I just don't know, Zach. Is it wrong to like him? Am I betraying my heart?"

I shook my head. "No, you aren't. You are just trying to move on. Cor has his own shit to deal with. It's not your baggage to carry. Let him figure it out and move on. You could have something special with Claude—you just have to give him a chance."

She took a deep breath. "I'm going to try. Or at least see where it all goes. He said he'll take it slow, and I told him I wasn't sure if I could feel any more for him. We're just testing the waters."

"It's a start at least."

She set the vegetables to the side. "I guess we have all the time in the world now since we're finally free of the burden of saving the world."

I frowned a little. "Do you want to go back out there?"

She shrugged. "We kind of abandoned it, didn't we?"

I shook my head. "It isn't ours to save, now is it? There are thousands upon thousands of other people in the world who can stand up to injustice. Have we seen any of them do that?"

Ellie shook her head. "Not in person, no."

"So why does it have to be us? Why do we have to risk our lives when no one risked their lives to help us?"

She bit her lip as if thinking. "I know what you say is right, Zach. But I just feel like... I don't know, like we have given up. And I don't want to give up on my home."

"Ellie, you are home. Being here with our people is home. Out there was nothing but prejudices and people trying to kill us. We're welcomed here. At least for the time being. Now, shouldn't we make the most of it? Your brother is so happy you are home, Ellie, as is Claude. We can keep living here until the end of time. The rest of the world can do whatever it wants. We're finally safe."

She slowly nodded. "You're right. We're safe and we're with friends and family. The world abandoned us a long time ago. I shouldn't keep trying to run back to it. This is a fresh start."

I wasn't sure if she meant the world or if she meant Cor. I wasn't going to say anything, however.

We went back to working on dinner. There were so many potatoes to cut and peel, but we were able to finish them all. As I worked, I wondered if Ellie was right, and I had every right to be mad at the people who hurt me when we were younger. It didn't feel like I should—not when they were so nice to us here. I couldn't even remember the names or faces of the people who'd picked on me. It was all a blur.

Were they all dead? Were they somewhere on Mu? Or were they in this camp? What if they started picking on me again? Where would we go? Was it right to leave and to take Ellie with me? After everything she had been through, was it right to take her away?

I pushed those thoughts into the back of my mind. It was no time to think about that. I hadn't received any sort of bullying, so I shouldn't be thinking about what-ifs. I had to live in the moment. I had to make friends and get to know these people. Then maybe, for once in my life, I'll feel as if I fit in.

CHAPTER XXII

Cor

A few days passed, and we began to get the hang of things, not to mention we finally got some furniture for our homes. My leg was beginning to heal, and I was able to stand on it for a while, and Gabe's shoulder was nearly healed. The two of us still had lookout duty and had learned all about the different gossip in the area. It was fantastic as I could definitely use it to my advantage, if need be, which was how I got what I wanted back when I was younger and living in Kaus.

As for Ellie and Claude... well... they seemed to be getting chummier each and every day. I should be happy for them. Ellie found someone she could count on, and I had someone as well. We could still be friends but have our own love lives.

It ate at me though, even though I should be happy with Gabe.

I could tell it bothered Gabe how much I was upset about Ellie, but how could I explain to him that I never saw a future without Ellie? That wouldn't be something he would want to hear—I knew. But that was how I felt. If there was anything I had learned in the past few years, it was that feelings were overrated.

Gabe was content here, at least. Everyone seemed to accept him, which I was glad for and a little suspicious. Perhaps they were just that hungry for other people that they didn't care. Or perhaps they are just waiting for the moment where they could attack him because he did something against Kausians, which would never happen. Gabe didn't have it in him to do anything mean, even if it were warranted.

No, the real traitor was me. And it was only a matter of time before they find out the truth.

I hadn't tried to run away again, mainly because I knew one of these lookouts would notice, and I wouldn't be able to make it down the mountain with a wound like I had currently. In these few days while I healed, I realized I could stay here. Byron and Krax got what was coming for them. They had both been tricked like they had tricked me. And there was no way I could stop Jonathan, so I shouldn't even think about it.

Gabe was happy, so that was what I knew I needed to focus on. He had been accepted here, which was less than anywhere else he had been. He got along with Ellie's brother and Claude, not to mention he got along with the lookout people as well. He could find a home here, as could I.

Or at least that was what I kept telling myself.

Ellie and I hadn't really talked since the night when we had that fight. She tried not to look at me anytime Claude sat close to her. Claude, on the other hand, always eyed me. It wasn't with a smirk or anything, but it was as if he was wondering what my response would be. He knew I still loved Ellie, but he had a point. I had to make up my mind, and she deserved better. I had to let her go.

As the days went by, I realized things were rather repetitive here, which was foreign to me. It wasn't a bad thing; it was just not something I was used to as I had never stayed in one place long enough to start doing the same things over and over again. Here, I woke up, got some breakfast, worked, had a snack for lunch, and then dinner was in the community area where people talked, laughed, played music, and danced. Those activities didn't last too late into the night as everyone had to pull their own weight in the community the next day if they were able.

It was as if disaster had caused these people to be the most well-organized community in the entire world.

Although we had a small community growing up, this was not how Kaus used to be. While we did try to look out for one another, there was bullying and arguments and fights. I had witnessed many shoot-outs while living in Kaus. But many people did what they could to survive. Now, however, everyone worked together to keep the community as a whole safe and sound. It was impressive, to say the least.

But there was still the rumor mill. The good ol' rumor mill.

"So," Rosa began. "You will not guess who I saw come out of Jackson's hut last night."

Jackson was one of the sons of the elders who helped run this community. I grinned. "Who?"

"Clara, who he was dancing with all night. Seems they are getting a little cozy."

Oh, to gossip about love life. How I missed those days. "No way. The two of them totally hated each other growing up."

"I know, right? It's so weird."

Gabe seemed totally confused as he glanced back and forth at the two of us, but he grinned at the interaction. He wouldn't know who the two people were, but gossip was gossip.

"Were they enemies or something?" Gabe asked.

I chuckled as I leaned in toward him. "When we were younger, we were all in elementary school with each other. Jackson used to pick on Clara. Pull her hair, stick bugs on her, stuff like that. She swore she would hate him forever and now…" I shrugged. "Looks like they don't hate each other anymore."

Gabe nodded as if he understood. "That's crazy."

It was good to have these types of normal interactions, if one called them normal. Gossip wasn't the healthiest thing in the world, but it made a community feel like a community. I hadn't known what I expected when Edmund led us to the camp, but I didn't expect everything to be going as smoothly as it was. This place seemed to have everything—more so than when we were young. And although everyone appeared to get along better than they had, there were still rumors that rippled through the people.

Ellie never cared for gossip, but I reveled in it. It was almost like a form of knowledge. No, not all the stories were true, but when you listened closely, you could tell the fake gossip from the real stories.

And knowledge was power. With the little things, you could tell how people were going to behave, and you could sometimes use it to your advantage. Or get into deep trouble with it. It could go either way.

Gabe stood up. "I'm going to go grab us some tea. Want anything else?"

We both shook our heads and watched as he left to retrieve the drinks.

"What about you? What's the story with you and Ellie? You used to be so close," Rosa commented as soon as Gabe was out of earshot.

I frowned a little. "What, are you going to use my story to fuel the gossip mill this week?"

She shrugged. "You could tell me, or I could just spread whatever story I want. Your choice."

She had a point there. I sighed. "Nothing really to tell. The two of us got separated, thought the other was dead, and moved on with our lives. I have Gabe here, whom I love with all my heart, and Ellie's got…" I hesitated before saying his name. "Claude."

"Yeah, we can all tell you still love her."

"But I have Gabe."

"Doesn't mean you can't still love her. The heart is capable of loving more than one person."

I stared down at my hands. "I still want her, yes, but I also don't want to dump Gabe. I'm happy with him. She deserves someone who will give her all his heart. I mean, Claude has loved her most of his life, just as I have. If anyone deserves her, it's him."

"If you really feel like that, that's fine. But have you ever thought about what Ellie wants? Maybe she wants you back but is too nice to ask you to dump Gabe."

"She made her decision. She accepted Claude's proposal to start dating. She wouldn't have done that if she didn't have any feelings for him."

"If you say so. I just think you are overthinking all this."

"Oh, do you now?"

Rosa leaned back. "I mean, why don't you see if they are open to more of a polyamorous thing? See if they care if you date both of them. They seem to get along, right?"

She had no idea how polyamorous Gabe's and my relationship was already. Which was another problem in this mix, not that I would be sleeping around with any other Kausians. That would get awkward real fast, not to mention I was sure if Edmund found out, he would kill me. He would see it as a betrayal to Ellie, just like he did for my dating Gabe.

"I don't think that will work, and it feels sort of selfish in a way. Ellie deserves someone's full heart."

"You can give your full heart to more than one person, believe me. I've been in a few poly relationships before. It's not as if you love one person more than another. But if you don't feel you can handle that type of dynamic, then definitely don't force yourself. I have seen that before, and it usually doesn't end pretty."

It was a thought I hadn't had, mainly because I didn't think either would go for it. Yes, I had sex with others while dating Gabe, but it was more like a business. It had nothing to do with love.

Gabe came back with the drinks. I smiled as I

took mine. "Thank you."

"You are most welcome. Did I miss anything?"

Rosa and I glanced at each other. "Nope," I answered. "Just sitting here enjoying the view."

I watched Gabe as he sipped his tea. Could I really have both? Or was that too selfish to ask for? Did it even matter now that Ellie had Claude? I sipped my own tea. I needed to live in the present, and this was where I was—with Gabe enjoying my smoky-flavored tea.

And yet I wanted more. I always wanted more.

CHAPTER XXIII

Ellie

It had been over a week since we first came to the camp, and we were settling in well. Or at least it seemed like we were. Cor was healing up fine and appeared to be less mad at me with each and every day that passed, and I was thankful for that. I didn't want to fight with him. Although we weren't exactly a couple anymore, I wanted to retain our friendship in whatever way possible.

Zach seemed to be getting more confident and less paranoid as the days went by. His nerves were going down, but I knew it would take time for him to feel comfortable around these people. He had been bullied for so long, and although I didn't recognize anyone who was an actual culprit, the prejudices that he had endured as a child were still there and it was hard to believe them to be gone in all these people. They also were accepting Gabe as one of their own, which was great for him since he hadn't fit in anywhere when he was growing up either. But I had to agree, it made me suspicious, and I kept my ears open for any comment about either of them. So far, however, there was nothing.

Then there was Claude. I could feel my cheeks warm at the thought of him. Maybe life with him wouldn't be as bad I thought, not that I thought it would be horrible or anything. I just thought, perhaps, it wouldn't be great. As a kid, he seemed like an older brother, especially since he and Edmund had always hung out. But he was sweet and caring, and things were a lot less awkward than I thought they would be. We were adults now, and a lot had happened in the past three years that changed us. It was great to learn about each other all over again, though I had a feeling my stories had surprised him more than his had me. And those were just the stories I was willing to share. A lot happened in the past three years that I didn't want to tell anyone—things Zach and I never mentioned to each other after they had happened.

Today I had foraging duty with Claude, which would be nice. Edmund said I couldn't have a gun again for a while—it was settlement policy when there was an accident. Zach commented to him that I was a lot more dangerous with a knife, which made my brother laugh. He knew it was probably true, as I was quite skillful at gutting and filleting fish as child.

I didn't know what to tell my brother when we got our moments alone together here and there. Did I tell him everything that had happened? Everything that I had done. I had told him we were bounty hunters, but that alone didn't completely explain the things that had happened. People were dead by my hand—ones that hadn't threatened me.

Well, I didn't quite pull the trigger, but I had handed them over to people who would, which in my mind was the same thing. I had to do it to survive, however. Perhaps they weren't innocent like they claimed they were to Zach and me. We had watched many men cry—beg us not to bring them in as they had a family and what not. The claimed their lives would be over. And we did nothing to save them.

Sometimes, late in the night, I could hear their voices.

Stuff like that was something Zach and I didn't like talking about. We just pushed it into the back of our minds and prayed it wouldn't haunt our nightmares.

Claude and I followed behind my brother and Zach as we ventured into the icy wilderness. It was quite cold when one went outside—they had done such a great job at keeping the settlement warm that I forgot we were in an icy desolate place. After a bit, our two parties split up so they could hunt in an area away from where we were going to forage.

Holding my gloved hand with his own, Claude

smiled to me and I back. Yeah, I could get used to this.

"So, are you liking life out here?" he asked. The sound of crunching snow under our boots was the only sound in this quiet forest.

"Yeah, I do. It's nice to finally find a home where we can relax. Zach and I never were really welcomed anywhere, not to mention we probably have had wanted posters in every town, big or small, at one point or another. Good thing they expire or get covered up with other wanted posters after a while. Otherwise, we would have had to go into hiding way earlier."

He shook his head. "I can't believe the two of you had to deal with that. It's crazy. And I bet you two didn't even do anything wrong."

I laughed. "I wouldn't go that far. I'm not as innocent as you make me out to be, Claude. Zach and I were bounty hunters, don't forget that. And if we weren't bounty hunting, we were probably stirring up some kind of trouble."

"Well, I'm glad you don't have to deal with any of that. You are safe here. And if for some reason you had to leave, I promise I'll always keep you safe."

I turned to him. "If I left here, you would leave too?"

He leaned in and kissed me on the lips. He backed up and nodded. "I thought you were dead, Ellie. I cared about you more than you could ever know. I don't want to lose you again. As long as you will have me, I will stay at your side."

I didn't know what to say. I was so used to being the one who had to chase the person they loved because they were the one who always ran when things got tough. Never did I imagine that someone would chase after me. Because, if I were honest, if I had tried to run at any point in my life, would Cor have gone looking for me like I had him?

My heart didn't want to know the answer.

Claude quickly kissed my lips again then turned back to the path. "Well, should we find some blackberries? Or maybe even huckleberries if we're lucky."

I nodded. "Yes please!"

I hadn't had huckleberries for a long time. They

only grew on the mountains, and although they did grow at the bottom of the snowline, not many people went out to pick them, which made them rather expensive. They were great on practically everything: syrup, ice cream, cake, muffins… My stomach started growling at the thought.

"Are you hungry already?" Claude laughed.

I shook my head. "No, I'm fine. I just started thinking about huckleberries and my stomach started demanding treats right away."

"You always did love them when your brother went and fetched some from the mountain. It was rare, though, since it was so far."

"Yeah, I remember waiting up for him. It was usually when you went out hunting and followed some deer all the way to the snowline, wasn't it?"

He nodded. "Yup. That seems like a lifetime ago."

"Yeah. It does."

We ventured to where Claude marked on his map we would be foraging and checking for huckleberries. As we approached the areas, I noted there were quite a few huckleberry shrubs. I smiled as if I were still a child finding a present their parents were hiding from them. We picked as many as we could, leaving some for the animals and for the bush to thrive.

I couldn't wait to see what the cooks for tomorrow were going to do with the load we brought back. Hopefully Edmund and Zach were having as much luck as we were having.

After a couple of hours of picking the huckleberries, the blackberries, and some greens from the forest, Claude turned to me.

"Hey, want to see something amazing?" He glanced up as if checking something before going on. "Yeah, we should be able to see it on a day like today."

"What is it?" I asked, smiling. What could be all the way out here?

He grabbed my hand. "It's easier if I show you. And I don't want to spoil the surprise."

I laughed as I followed him up the hill a little bit. I was tired, but I didn't complain. I wanted to know what he wanted to show me.

We made it to the top of the hill, and I gasped at

the scene in front of me. I could see almost all the zones of Mu below. All except for the Sirian Zone, of course, since it was underwater. I could see the ocean in which it lay, however.

"This is beautiful," I whispered.

"It's one of my favorite spots. It's of course only visible on clear days such as this one, which can sometimes be rare. In the winter we won't be able to see anything, but on a summer day like this, it can be crystal clear."

Everything looked so small and peaceful, with clusters of towns here and there and roads connecting them all, but I knew the truth. None of those areas were peaceful. My eyes glazed over each and every zone. Then it came to the big empty desert that was Kaus.

My heart sank. Although I had gone to where Kaus once stood before, seeing it from such a distance was still heartbreaking. Claude put his arm around me.

"It's fine now. Our people still live. We're alive."

I slowly nodded. "Yeah, I suppose we are."

"Maybe one day we'll return."

I shook my head. "I've been back there. It's a barren wasteland. There is no way anything can live out there. Not after what those missiles did to the soil, not that it was in great shape to begin with."

"That's what they said about the mountains, and yet here we are."

That was fair. I turned to him. "Thank you for showing me. It really puts everything in perspective, you know?"

He nodded. "It really does. It also makes you realize how precious life is and how we should cherish every moment."

I smiled. That was definitely true.

"Should we head back?" he asked. "I'm sure your brother is wondering where I whisked you away to."

I nodded and turned to look out at Mu once more, not just to take in the beauty but to get a mental map of the area between us and the rest of the world. Now I knew exactly where I was on this mountain. Just in case.

"Yes, let's."

CHAPTER XXIV

Gabe

For once in my life I felt accepted somewhere.

It was a strange feeling. I didn't quite know what to do with myself. I was still surprised that a group of people who had been harmed as much as the Kausians had would be willing to let in an outsider like me. Perhaps they didn't want to let me leave for fear that I would tell other people about this place, and they were too kind to kill me on the spot.

Or perhaps they were lonely and wanted to interact with more people. Either way, I was fitting in and getting to know everyone here, and they all seemed like a good bunch of people.

And Cor seemed to be enjoying himself more now that we had settled. It was definitely rocky at first—I could tell. Seeing all these people after so long must have been hard for him, especially since he felt responsible for the destruction of their hometown. But whatever he and Ellie argued about must have sunk in as he started to open up more to people around him.

Well, not open up about everything but at least he was trying to be friendly to people.

His leg was almost healed, but Rosa recommended at least another couple of days of being the lookout. I, on the other hand, had healed up quite nicely and was tasked to help clean the animal cave that wasn't too far away. And it stank. Really bad. But after a while, I felt as if the smell either had dissipated a little or I had grown used to it. Either way, my nose stopped burning.

The Kausians had chickens and a couple of

milking cows, along with some ducks and pigs. I had never worked with such animals since, well, we didn't have them in the Sirian Zone. Even if we did, I doubted a prince like me would have had to do the work I was doing now. For all I knew, we did have something similar, and I was too sheltered to know about it. I had left before I was an adult, after all.

I used the broom to sweep out the debris, mainly poop and uneaten food. I tried my best not to vomit or make disgusted sounds. I didn't want to seem like a pampered prince, but it was just so gross. I definitely would prefer any other job than this, even hunting.

One of the other people helping me clean and feed the animals was the elder Mae. She laughed when she saw my face. "I was wondering if you were going to be able to handle this work. To be honest, I signed up myself when I saw you were listed for this task today. Just to see if a prince such as yourself was capable."

I blushed a little. "Thank you for the confidence."

She chuckled. "Well, not many people in all of Mu are accustomed to working with barn animals. Good for you for not complaining or arguing even if your face says it all."

"Everyone plays a part in society. No work is more important than the other. I'll do what I can to help you all even if it is work I'm not accustomed to."

"That's the spirit, Gabe. I'm glad you are so open-minded. It's too bad you couldn't have ruled the Sirian Zone. You would have made a great leader."

I smiled. "Thank you. That means a lot. Although my view on the world may have been different if I didn't grow up the way I did."

Mae nodded. "I understand that. A lot of Kausians would not have accepted you if you had walked into Kaus as you are. But since we had dealt with our own prejudices, had our own land destroyed, we can tell you are genuine and someone to trust." She shoveled up some more of the grossness that covered the floor of the cave. "Tell me, how are you liking it here?"

"I like it a lot, actually. I know it will get harder in the winter, but I feel like you all have the hang of it here. After everything that has happened, I'm glad you are able to find a somewhat safe and secure home away from all the chaos and destruction. And no one even knows you are out here, not even my father."

"You can say that again. I'm glad we have so many people who can work hard and don't put up a fuss. Sure, there are squabbles and fights of course but nothing compared to what's out there or what it was like in Kaus before the attack. Although a lot of people lost their lives that day, I have always wondered if it were for the better. Like you said, we're a lot more well off than we have been."

I wasn't sure what to say to that. I could understand that, though. A lot had happened, but it led me to Cor and the others. Would I have had it any differently? We had suffered so much loss but had gained a lot in return. I wasn't sure what to think any more.

"Well, anyway, I'm glad you are able to find a home here. The others were hesitant to let you stay, but I could tell you were truthful."

I smiled a little. It was heartwarming to hear that someone took a chance on me instead of presuming I was something without getting to know me. Not many took the trouble.

"Thank you. That means a lot."

"And I'm glad you took a chance on one of our own even though you probably have heard a lot of horrible things about our kind."

I looked at her quizzically. "Do you mean Cor?"

She nodded. "And Ellie and Zach of course, but you and Cor are an item, are you not? So you took a chance there."

"Oh yeah. I suppose I did. I mean, he was in quite the predicament when I found him. He didn't seem like he could do much harm."

Mae laughed. "Cor in a predicament? I can't imagine there had been an instance where he isn't in some kind of trouble."

I grinned. "Well, now that you mention it… Sounds like he was like that as a child as well."

"You can say that again. He, Zach, and Ellie always wound up in some kind of trouble. They were lucky no one killed them in a different nation. I know plenty have probably tried."

"And they try and try again," I said. "Cor never seemed to be able to go anywhere without someone wanting to hurt him. While most times he did do something to piss someone off, many times that wasn't the case."

"That's what it's like to be a Kausian. You always have to be wary of others. Even if you didn't do anything wrong, there might be someone out there who will target you just because of what you are. So, some people might think they might as well as do something wrong to receive such treatment. I have a feeling that's how those three feel."

I had never thought of it that way. I could understand where that type of thinking came in. If you were always seen as a criminal, why not do something to deserve that kind of punishment? I had always been seen as an outsider in the eyes of my people, so perhaps that was why I ran away? So I would be an outsider of sorts.

"But I'm glad they finally found this place and

that they were able to survive out there. I know it had to have been hard," Mae commented.

I gestured around. "Setting all this up had to have been difficult as well. I can't even imagine how much time it took and what lengths you all went to before you were able to find a groove for it all."

Mae nodded. "Yes, it took a while, but we had each other, which made it easier. We could support each other and keep going, and we knew we couldn't give up without impacting someone else. Those three though… They didn't have that type of community, and yet they were able to keep going."

I never had a community I could lean on either, so I understood what she was saying for Cor and the others. This whole place was like some foreign idea to me. A community that accepted everyone was truly rare.

"One of the others mentioned there were scouts out in the towns. I thought you mentioned no one leaves here."

She grinned a little. "I didn't want you all to believe you could just leave. The scouting missions take a lot of time to prepare. It was the only way we were able to get all these supplies. We were careful and went to different towns for different things. To be honest, when Cor has always been one to… go missing for a bit when he was young, and I didn't want him to get any ideas. He thought no one would notice, but his parents were always worried sick. We also weren't sure if we could trust you all. Maybe in a few months, after the winter, you can help with a mission."

I shook my head. "No, I think that wouldn't be a good idea. We are probably on wanted posters in every bar known to man."

"Right, well then I guess you all are stuck here for the time being."

"I can't complain. Well, other than when cleaning after these animals."

Mae laughed as we went back to work. It was great to be able to talk to her again as she seemed like a great leader but still accessible to everyone. Most leaders I knew, it was hard for anyone to talk to them, and they had to go through a bunch of hoops to only be denied a face-to-face meeting.

I helped finish cleaning out the animal pens, and

Mae and I fed the animals and gathered eggs. I enjoyed these things a lot more than cleaning the stalls. Mae even taught me how to milk a cow, which was one of the strangest things I had ever done. Who even thought to try this? And why did it taste so good?

"If Ellie and Claude are able to get some huckleberries, perhaps we can make some ice cream to go with it," Mae commented as she lifted her pails.

My eyes widened. "Ice cream? Really?"

"Yes, it is a treat we like to make at least once a week. Goes very well with some berries. Do you like ice cream, Gabe?"

"Do the two stars shine bright in the sky?" I asked with a smile.

"I'll take that as an enthusiastic yes. Well then, shall we go check on the others?"

I nodded. "Yes, let's."

CHAPTER XXV

Zach

Everything was going smoothly. We were acclimating to being part of the community, and it seemed like things were almost perfect here. Everyone got along here and there wasn't much fighting, other than just typical arguing that can happen between two people, but it all appeared to work out in the end. Even Ellie and Cor were working out their issues, or at least they were talking again. Her and Claude have been growing close, and her brother was more than happy for her to be dating someone other than Cor.

But it felt as if something was going to go wrong at any second.

Was that just my paranoia? Had I grown accustomed to there always being a turn for the worst that I assumed the worst for everything? We were happy here—we had been happy for over a week now after two weeks of complete torture. We were safe and sound, and yet…

Yet I just knew something bad was going to happen.

Ellie had shot Cor, but that wasn't anything too terrible. But I felt like something much worse was going to happen. Would Jonathan find us maybe? Would he search the mountains for us? Did he already have control over all of Kaus already? Was it too late to stop him?

I shook my head. We weren't in a position to stop him. We weren't powerful like he was. There were plenty of others who could say or do something, but they hadn't. Instead, they let him gain the power he had now, and he was going to take over everything and make humans the ruling race over it all.

Would things be for the better after it was all over? Probably not—not when it was some conniving, racist asshole that was ruling. Things would probably get a lot worse before any good change would happen, which would be after our lifetime. But we were safe currently. We could keep living out here and be happy. What more could we ask for?

Ellie and I were on guard duty today. Although I felt like it was a little bit overkill, I completely understood why they always had guards posted. We had lost our home once, and I doubted any of us wanted to lose it again. There were enemies that wanted all of us dead and if even a whisper about this place got out, I had a feeling an army would be sent.

That is, once things settled down. I had a feeling Jonathan had his hands full between taking over for his brother and dealing with the Silurians.

Cor and Gabe were on guard duty while they

healed from their wounds, but since Cor's leg was better and Gabe's arm was completely healed, they had new jobs as all the tasks here were on a rotating basis. Cor was helping with laundry today with Gabe. It wasn't the worst task—laundry was rather relaxing compared to a lot of things here, but it got tedious after a while.

Just like guard duty.

"I spy something tall," I said out of the blue. I needed to do something to pass the time.

Ellie rolled her eyes. "Is it a tree?"

"How did you know?" I grinned.

She rolled her eyes again. "You just think you are so funny, Zach."

"I don't think—I know I am."

She pulled out her binoculars. "Doesn't seem to be much movement out there. I don't even see any animals."

"Yeah, we don't get to see too much out here doing this, but we want to make sure the camp is safe," a man by the name of Jackson commented. He was also on guard duty as there was always three or four people assigned to the task. He sipped his tea. "At least we get to chill here and don't have to clean up the animal cave."

Ah yes. The animal cave. Ellie and I had already done that this week. It brought back memories of having to help with her parents' farm. I wasn't sure if I felt nostalgic or sad to have to be shoveling crap all over again.

"And get to drink tea." Ellie raised her cup to her lips. "I missed Kausian tea. I can't believe you are able to gather everything you need for it."

"Only in the summer. We send some parties to go collect stuff, but they have to be extra careful not to arouse suspicion from the local government or any rogue parties. Speaking of which, I think there should be a party coming back shortly. We will want to keep any eye out for them," Jackson explained.

Ellie nodded to me. "How will the two of us know what they look like?"

"They will be wearing a piece of purple fabric over their jackets. And that's why none of you are out here on your own. Got to get used to being able to spot who is part of the community or at least know everyone's faces. That will happen over time and when everyone is back."

We both nodded. That made perfect sense. I took a deep breath as I glanced back out at the snowy forest below us. Would someone show up today? Or would it just be a lot of hanging around and watching the snow fall around us?

I didn't mind the snow now that we had a nice place to stay. I could get used to it all. Yes, it was cold out here, but in the cave, it was a moderate temperature. I didn't know how cold it would get in the winter, but I had a feeling it would be a lot better than just a shack the four of us would have been living in. We had food, friends, and a place to sleep. It was all we really needed.

Which is why I felt like something was going to happen. Nothing was ever this perfect for us.

"Is something wrong?" Ellie whispered as she glanced at me.

I shook my head. "No, not really. Everything is perfect. Especially this tea."

She glanced down at her cup. "You can say that again. But I get what you mean. It is perfect, which is why you looked worried, right?"

I nodded.

"I feel paranoid too. It has been a long, long time since we stayed anywhere this long. Something always happened. Someone always showed up wanting to kill us. But, honestly, Zach, I think we are fine here. I think for once in our lives we are okay."

I gave her a light smile, but I still couldn't believe it. I just prayed we would have a little more time to stay like this.

Some time passed, and the two suns were about to set in the distance. I stood up and stretched. "Looks like no one is coming back today."

"Perhaps not," Jackson commented. "As I said, it would be sometime soon. With all the safeguards we have, the exact day of return is not easily calculated. I just hope something didn't happen to them this time around."

"Has something happened in the past?" Ellie asked.

Jackson shook his head. "Nothing horrible.

People have been attacked by bandits when they are on the road traveling, but they only took some of their supplies before running off. But you never know if someone might get captured. That's our worst fear. So far, so good, though. Bandits don't spread rumors since they want to stay hidden as well. But if someone gets arrested and questioned, there is always the possibility they will leak information and the nations that attacked us will find out the truth. That we survived."

We both nodded. We knew that feeling all too well. We had been captured, attacked, mugged, what have you, multiple times. Sometimes, no matter how careful you are, someone would decide you are their next target.

"How many people were in the party?" Ellie asked as she held up her binoculars.

"Four. Any more would raise suspicion in towns. You know how other zones are about seeing a group of Kausians together," Jackson answered.

"Oh, I know. They raise suspicion even when there is just one of us," Ellie continued. "But what if there are five people in the group?"

Jackson's eyes narrowed. "What do you mean?"

Ellie pointed. "Down there. I see a group coming, but it looks like there is a fifth person. The four are wearing the purple you mentioned. The fifth person appears injured, however. Maybe they found someone?"

Jackson stood up and grabbed his binoculars. I stared out at the forest. I could see movement, but they were still quite far away, and I didn't have any binoculars.

"That's them. The other person appears to be Kausian as well. They must have found a survivor. That is rare but not unheard of, as you know."

I wondered who it could have been and whether or not it was someone we knew. Ellie and I glanced at each other. The Kausians on the outside were a bit different than the ones here. First off, they knew a bit more of what was going on in the different zones. It just depended on where they were from.

It took a good hour before the group reached the gates where we were waiting for them. Jackson confirmed who they were, and they led the man to the infirmary as his leg was severely injured.

"The two of you stay here and make sure the camp stays safe. I'll help them get to where they need to go," Jackson said as he helped the injured man.

I nodded and turned to Ellie. Ellie appeared as if she had seen a ghost. I had never seen her so stricken.

"What's wrong?" I asked.

She shook her head. "It can't be. Out of all the Kausians they could have found…"

"What do you mean?"

"Zach… that's the Kausian that killed Gabe's mother." She turned to the door. "I have to go tell Cor and Gabe. Cor needs to get out of here."

"Wait, Ellie, what does this have to do with Cor?"

She turned to me with tears in her eyes. "That man knows the truth, and he was the one who beat Cor until he passed out in the Sirian Zone. He knows everything and the moment he sees Cor, he is going to tell them all the truth. I can't let that happen, Zach. I just… I can't."

I frowned as I watched her run inside the camp.

There went our little happily-ever-after.

CHAPTER XXVI

Cor

I could get used to this.

Those were thoughts I never believed I could think. For once, I felt as if I could belong somewhere and be content. I hadn't thought about revenge for an entire day. Maybe Ellie was right. Maybe I could move on.

I never thought it possible—I always believed I would have to keep running.

Gabe went to deliver some of the sheets, so I found myself alone in the laundry area. Usually when I was alone like this, I would think of ways I could escape. But now, I didn't think about those things. I was finally free.

As I folded the last sheet for the day, I heard the sound of boots hitting the ground quickly. There was someone running toward me. I turned to find Ellie, disheveled, and her face as white as snow.

Yup. It was all too good to be true. I knew it.

Ellie reached me and appeared as if she were going to collapse.

I held on to her arm to keep her up. "Whoa, Ellie. What's wrong? What happened?"

"That Kausian," she managed to say. "The one from the Sirian Zone. They found him and brought him here. He must have escaped during the chaos. You need to get out of here."

My eyebrows furrowed. "What guy?" Then it hit me. She meant the Kausian that Byron had attack me. The one who knew what I had done. The one who would tell everyone that I had destroyed Kaus and hunted our kind for Drax. I covered my mouth.

"There's no way… Byron would have killed him to tie loose ends."

"He must have been more focused on us, and so the Kausian escaped. Then before he got a chance to search for him, Jonathan killed him. But you have to get out of here. The moment he sees you, he'll tell everyone everything. Zach and I are the ones guarding the gate right now. This is your only chance to get out of here."

I knew she was right. I needed to get out of here. Any trust these people had would leave the moment he tells them what happened. They would arrest and kill me, and I couldn't blame them. I had hoped that maybe the truth wouldn't come out, or at least not for a while. I had finally found somewhere I belonged and now it was gone just like that. It just wasn't fair, but there was no way I could stay. This was my only chance.

"Let me grab my things. I need weapons and supplies."

"What about Gabe?" she asked.

I opened my mouth, then closed it. Did I drag him along to a place where his father might find him? Or did I leave him here with people he didn't know as well? He was getting along with everyone here, I couldn't argue that. But that didn't mean he would want to be here by himself. He might have Ellie and Zach, but he had only just met them a month ago. I rubbed my face.

"I don't know."

"He should know you are leaving," Ellie said.

"But there isn't enough time for a discussion on whether he should come with me, now is there?" I countered.

Ellie seemed to hesitate. "What... what about me?"

I stared at her. "What do you mean what about you?"

"Did it occur to you to ask me to run away with you?" She whispered the question.

We were silent for a long moment. To be honest, I did want her to run away with me, but she had Claude. There was no way I could let her come with, and there was still Gabe I had to think of. Besides, it didn't seem like there was still a "we" that would involve us running away together.

"You have Claude," I finally said.

"Right. I guess I do."

I wanted to tell her that I always loved her and that I did in fact want to run away with her, but I couldn't do that to her. This wasn't her problem—it was mine.

I turned toward my hut. "I have to hurry. Gabe is delivering some of the laundry to residents. He could be anywhere. I don't have time to explain it all to him. He will be better off staying here."

"You don't know that."

"Oh, but I do. Jonathan will do anything to hunt him down. This is the safest place he can stay."

Ellie shook her head. "Whatever. Do what you want. I'll be at the gate waiting for you."

She hurried off in the other direction, and I went to my hut. I didn't have much, but I wanted to grab my gun and knife and another jacket for the cold. It was going to be dark soon, and I didn't want to freeze to death out there. I also grabbed some matches if I needed to start a fire although that would make it so if any Kausian knew I had run away, they could find me. I would have to just keep moving through the night.

I pulled out my engagement ring that was still in my pocket. What did I do with this? I had always kept it because I had hoped, somewhere deep in my heart, Ellie still wanted to be with me. But now she'd moved on and she made it clear that I was selfish and didn't think about her the way I should. I didn't deserve to keep this. I set it down on the table in my hut and turned away. She had Claude now. She could be happy without me. I didn't have to worry about her any longer.

I couldn't believe this was all happening. It wasn't fair. None of this was fair. Why did it have to be that Kausian? Why couldn't it have been someone who didn't know the truth? Why did my past continue to haunt me?

Grabbing a bag, I hurried to where some Kausians were setting up for dinner. When the cooks weren't looking, I put some food in the bag and grabbed a container of water. It should be able to last me until morning or at least until I could get down the mountain, whenever that would be. If I had to take a guess, I was at least three days walking distance to the snowline, and then some more to the nearest city. At least I knew how to forage.

I made my way to the entrance of the cave, hoping no one would notice me—hoping the Kausian hadn't said anything yet. Odds were he wouldn't talk about how he killed the queen of the Sirian Zone, but one never knew.

Ellie and Zach were waiting for me. I still couldn't believe all this was happening and how fast I needed to get out of there. I had finally decided not to run away—decided I wanted to be in their lives for the rest of my days, and now I was forced to leave because of some stupid Kausian who had done as much destruction to a zone as I had. But I had a feeling he would be forgiven quicker than I would be. He didn't kill our own kind.

Ellie pointed down the mountain. "If you go straight down here, take a left about a mile out, you will go straight down the mountain. I saw it with my own eyes a couple of days ago."

I nodded. "Right."

We all stood there in silence. The suns were about to set. I needed to move fast in order to get a good distance before it was pitch black out there.

"Good luck," Ellie finally said.

I knew I needed more than luck to keep me alive out there. I took a deep breath and started to step forward.

"Wait," Ellie said as she grabbed my arm and turned me around. She kissed me hard. I about dropped my things. As quickly as she moved to me, she moved away.

Maybe I should have asked her to run away with me. I glanced at Zach, who was giving a disapproving frown.

"Never change, Zach. And keep Ellie safe, okay?"

He nodded. "Stay safe, Cor."

I didn't say anything because I knew there was no way I was going to be safe out there. But if I stayed here, I had a feeling everyone was going to try to kill me. It was probably safer out there than it was here right now. I took a deep breath and embarked on a journey that I knew would change everything I had grown to love.

CHAPTER XXVII

Ellie

I watched as he descended the mountain. This wasn't fair. None of this was fair.

But the moment that Kausian saw Cor, he was going to tell everyone the truth. Cor would be tortured and killed. I couldn't let that happen. Not after what I saw that Kausian do to Cor in the Sirian Zone. He didn't deserve that.

I turned to Zach, who was frowning.

"What is it?" I asked.

"Was that kiss necessary? Aren't you dating Claude?"

I took a breath and let it out slowly. "It wasn't like that. I was saying goodbye. There is a possibility we won't ever see him again, Zach."

"I guess. But that seemed more like a desperate kiss than anything. Like you wanted him to take you with him."

Was that true? Had I wanted Cor to take me with him? I did comment to Cor how he didn't ask me to go with him, but was it because I wanted to go or because I wanted to see if any thought of me crossed his mind? I couldn't deny that the thought of the two of us on the run together had gone through my mind.

But he also left Gabe behind.

Did he not love Gabe as much as I thought? Did I still have a chance with Cor? No, I knew I shouldn't be thinking thoughts like that. I was with Claude. He made me happy. He put me before himself at times. He made sure I was well cared for. He wouldn't leave me like Cor had in the past and was doing right now.

Then why did my heart still yearn for Cor?

Cor disappeared into the thick forest just as Jackson appeared again. I let out a breath of relief.

"Did I miss anything?" Jackson asked.

Zach and I shook our heads. "No. Nothing."

"That's good. It seems that Kausian was really shook up. The doctor was able to give him a sedative. I wonder what happened to that poor guy. The council will have a lot of questions once he comes to."

Zach and I glanced at each other. At least that would keep people off Cor's tail for a while.

We knew exactly what happened to that Kausian—he'd had to deal with Byron. He had been captured and forced to kill a leader of a zone.

I wondered how much he was going to confess. Would he tell them what he did or was forced to do? It wasn't as if we were quite straightforward with everything we had been involved in. We didn't mention what Cor had done or how Zach was forced to transform into the leader of the Silurians and made them commit a terrorist attack. There were a lot of secrets all around. He might just say he was attacked for being a Kausian and leave it at that. It wasn't far from the truth.

"The two of you can go back inside," Jackson said. "I can stay here until the night shift comes. It's no problem. You had to cover for me for a bit."

I glanced at Zach. This would give us some time to talk to Gabe and tell him what had happened.

"That would be great," I said. "Thank you."

With that, Zach and I went back into the camp and searched for Gabe. According to Cor, he was delivering laundry to people while Cor had been finishing everything up.

"We don't want to seem like we're in a hurry or else we'll attract suspicion," I commented as I glanced around at the people who were getting ready for dinner.

Zach nodded. "I was about to say the same thing."

As we rounded a corner, we found Claude heading in our direction. He smiled when he saw me, and I did the same. He hurried over and gathered me up and twirled me around.

"How was your day, my love?" he asked as he set me down.

I shrugged. "It was the same ol', same ol'." That was not a lie, which was probably the worst part. "The group of Kausians who went down for supplies brought in a refugee. Seems he was hurt and in a lot of pain."

"I heard about that. I was working in the infirmary when they brought him in. I hope he wakes up and is able to explain what happened."

Part of me hoped he wouldn't wake up and that I could go look for Cor and bring him back. "Yeah, hopefully."

"Well, I got to go finish up helping Edmund. See you at dinner?"

I nodded. "Yes, see you."

With that, he left us.

Zach said, "I wonder what he is going to say when he finds out you helped Cor run away from here."

I let out a breath. They were going to know we had something to do with that since we were at the guard post. "Yeah, about that. What should we say?"

"People are going to be suspicious that he was able to sneak past the front area. They will know it was us," Zach said.

"That is what I was thinking. Should we say he told us he was going to get a breather and then just never came back?"

"I think we should say that he told us he couldn't stay here so we let him go, just like any friend would. But that we didn't know why he couldn't stay here."

I nodded. "That sounds believable. Then we can claim we didn't know about anything that had happened other than all the stuff that has happened in the past few weeks."

"We'll just have to make sure Gabe is on the same page."

Telling Gabe was not going to be the easiest thing to do. I knew what it was like to be left behind by Cor. It wasn't fun. "Yeah… let's go find him."

Zach and I checked where the laundry was done first in case Gabe had already made it back there.

Lucky for us, he was there and seemed a bit flustered.

"Have you two seen Cor? I'm not sure where he went. He was here just a minute ago but now there is no sign of him."

I put my hand on his shoulder and squeezed it. "There is something we need to talk about. Can we go to your hut?"

Gabe nodded absentmindedly. I had a feeling he knew what could have happened since I was asking to talk in private. We made our way to his hut and sat Gabe down on the bed.

"An injured Kausian was brought to camp. He… he knows what Cor did. Cor had to make a run for it before word came out of what happened," I explained, not beating around the bush.

Gabe stared at me. "He… ran? Like, he's gone? Didn't even wait to ask me if I wanted to go with him? Just poof—vanished?"

Ellie shook her head. "He wanted to wait, but he didn't want to risk it and he didn't want to risk your life. He knew if he took you anywhere else in Mu that your father would find you. He said you were safest here."

"That wasn't for him to decide!" Gabe exclaimed.

I had never seen Gabe angry, and a lot of stuff had happened in the past few weeks. I jumped back a little, startled. I glanced at the door, hoping no one overheard him. "Well, Cor likes making his own decisions without taking anyone else into consideration. You probably know that already though." I sat down next to him. "I'm sorry it has come to this. I wish there was an easier way."

He shook his head. "No, I'm going to go after him! I don't want to stay here without him!"

Zach held out his hand before Gabe could get up. "Cor's right, though. You are safest here. Just sleep on it. If you want to go after him and try to find him, we will help you. But first rest a little. Besides, it's dangerous going down the mountain at night."

"Will Cor be okay? He will be going down the mountain at night."

"Cor can handle it," I said. "He is far more well equipped to make a run for it. I assumed the times he went gathering and you were watching out for people he'd made a mental map in case he needed to run. I also gave him directions."

"He better be fine. I want him in perfect condition before I punch him."

I knew that feeling all too well. "He will be fine. We Kausians are strong. Now, do you want to go to dinner or want us to bring it to you? If you come with us, we will have to tell people Cor had a headache or something and retired early for the day."

Gabe took a deep breath as if trying to calm himself down. "I'll go with you. But first I want to know who is the Kausian that came in? Is he a friend of yours? How did he know about Cor?"

Zach and I glanced at each other. Zach was first to speak. "You should know the truth. The Kausian that came in was the one that Byron used in the Sirian Zone. Byron told him what Cor did so that he could torture Cor."

Gabe frowned. "The one in the Sirian Zone? You mean the one that killed my mother? The one that transformed as me and made my people believe I had murdered my own mother?"

I slowly nodded. "Which was all orchestrated by Byron. Just like how Cor destroyed Kaus because of Byron. And how Zach was used to start a war with the Silurians. The Kausian was just a puppet of Byron's. It's because of Byron that everything happened."

Gabe slowly nodded. "Right. I know." He was silent for a moment then said, "Will the two of you give me a moment? Then I'll join you for dinner."

Zach and I started for the door when I spotted something on the table. It was a wooden ring. I grabbed it and held it in my hand for a moment.

He had left this behind. He had left our ring behind. Perhaps our story truly was at a close.

I tucked what was once a symbol of our love into my pocket and followed Zach out the door. It was time to move forward. I couldn't keep living in the past.

CHAPTER XXVIII

Gabe

The man who killed my mother was inside this camp.

I knew it was Byron's fault as well as my father's that my mother was dead. They had both used us for their sick game. They wanted power, and they didn't care who was killed along the way. My father was going to use me and my mother to take over the Sirian Zone when the time was right, then he was going to murder me and take over. It was his fault and Byron's fault.

Joining Ellie and Zach for dinner, I tried to act as normal as possible. It was hard, as one doesn't know what their normal is until they have to try to act like everything was fine. Then everything felt wrong.

Because everything was wrong.

Cor was gone. I was alone again. I had Ellie and Zach, of course, and all these people, but that wasn't the same. And to top it off, the man responsible for my mother's death was here. Was he going to get to stay here? Would I have to see him every day? Or would they accept him and say it wasn't his fault? Should I tell someone what I knew, or would that put Cor's life in jeopardy?

I didn't have an answer for any of it.

All I knew was that I just needed to get through this dinner so I could go back and break down on my bed and figure out what I would do next. I didn't want to think about it here. I just wanted to eat.

Ellie was talking with Claude, laughing and

letting him keep her arm around her. I wanted that. I wanted Cor.

We were finally happy. We were finally free of all the burdens we were carrying. But apparently we weren't. Apparently it was only a matter of time until it all exploded in our faces yet again.

Could I really stay here among these people without him? Sure, I was friends with Ellie and Zach, but that wasn't the same. I wanted to be with Cor.

I should have known he was going to leave me. We should have discussed it together. I should have at least been able to say goodbye.

Was it wrong of me to be glad he didn't take Ellie with him? That she too was left behind? Was this what she felt like all those years ago as well? To find he had moved on?

No, he hadn't moved on. He was just running away from his problems like he always did. He would be back. He had to be back. Or I would go find him.

But where would I even look? It wasn't as if I could ask around different parts when he would be hiding from my father, not to mention I didn't want to be found out by him. I didn't know what to do.

It was all the Kausian's fault.

If this Kausian didn't do as Byron said—if he had rebelled and hadn't killed my mother, it would have all been fine. If he hadn't been rescued and brought here, then Cor would still be here. We would be happy. We would be free. It was because of him that I found myself all alone. It was because of him my mother was dead and my love was gone.

Dinner finished up, and I headed back to my hut. As I lay on my bed, staring at the ceiling, the thoughts kept circling around in my mind. That Kausian was at the bottom of most of my problems. I had to do something.

Getting up out of bed, I knew I had to put an end to all of this.

I grabbed one of the knives that Cor had left behind. I was glad there was some sort of weapon still in the drawer, otherwise I would have had to sneak into Ellie and Zach's house, and I had a feeling Ellie was not a heavy sleeper. I gripped the handle tightly and headed out the door before I could talk myself out of what I was about to do.

It was quiet out, as everyone was asleep. It wasn't as if there was any sort of guards inside since everyone got along here. I made my way to the infirmary.

And there he was—sleeping in a cot. The man who had killed my mother.

I squeezed the handle of the knife and walked over to where the Kausian lay. I stared down at him.

Was this the right thing? Would killing this person really bring back my mother? Would it bring back Cor? Cor had already run away. There was no way to find him.

I raised my knife.

But justice would be served. This man had destroyed everything I had loved. He deserved to die.

"What are you doing!" A voice came from behind me.

I dropped the knife and turned around to find Dr. Pheles standing there.

"I… um…it's not."

"Someone help! I need someone to be restrained!"

"Please, you don't understand," I started, but it was too late. A couple of men came in and grabbed me.

I had really messed up this time.

CHAPTER XXIX

Zach

We awoke to Edmund in our home.

"Ellie, Zach, you need to get up. Your Sirian friend is in a lot of trouble," Edmund said as he shined his lantern in our faces.

I groaned.

"What are you talking about?" Ellie asked as she rubbed her eyes.

"He tried to murder the Kausian that came in

yesterday. And we can't find Cor."

Both Ellie and I sat up quickly, smacking each other in the head. We both moaned in pain but got up to follow Edmund.

Gabe had tried to kill the Kausian.

I couldn't blame him. It was the Kausian that had killed his mother. It wasn't like Cor when he had given the codes and didn't know what Byron was going to do with them. No, the Kausian had used his own two hands to murder Gabe's mother.

Just like I had when Byron made me appear like the Silurian. I had instructed the Silurians to kill those people. Their blood was on my hands as well.

I pushed back those thoughts as we made our way to the infirmary. We should have made him stay with us last night. We should have kept an eye on him. But I never would have imagined him to try to murder someone out of revenge. He didn't seem like the type.

"Ellie," I whispered. "What are we going to do?"

She shook her head. "I don't know yet. Give me a bit to figure it all out."

"What are we going to say about Cor?"

"I don't know."

We arrived at the infirmary to find Gabe bound and his eyes filled with tears. It didn't seem that he actually went through with anything. They must have found him before he tried to kill the Kausian. I didn't know which of those two scenarios would be worse as he was in a lot of trouble either way.

Mae, Dr. Pheles, and Claude were there as well. I took a deep breath, trying to calm myself down. This was not going to end well.

"Do either of you know why your friend tried to kill this man? He isn't saying anything."

Ellie and I glanced at each other. Before I could tell them anything, Ellie spoke up.

"He is the Kausian who killed the Sirian queen. I… told him it was that Kausian and that we should talk to him in the morning to see if we can get any information on Jonathan and what he is doing in Mu. Gabe was only acting out of revenge, like what any of you would do," she explained.

"You should have come forward with this information earlier. We would have handled it better and wouldn't be in this position," Mae stated.

Ellie nodded. "I'm sorry, ma'am."

"No." Mae rubbed her forehead. "Do you care to explain where Cor is right now."

Shit. This wasn't going to end well.

Ellie shook her head. "I'm not sure, ma'am."

"Really? You have no idea?"

Ellie glanced over to Claude who was frowning at her. "He… he ran away. Last night. I'm not sure why."

"When the two of you were at guard."

Ellie and I both nodded. I didn't know what to say. This was all going to shit.

"Did it not occur to you to think to ask him what he was running away from?" Mae asked.

"It's Cor. He is always running away from something. He can't sit still," Ellie explained.

Mae shook her head. "No, you know something else—something that could endanger all of us. Now tell me what it is before I decide to throw you all out of here with no supplies to deal with the cold out there."

Ellie looked away. There was one thing the two of us had in common—we both couldn't tell them what Cor had done. But if we didn't talk, then we were going to be held responsible for everything.

So I spoke up. "Cor was the one who gave the codes to the outsiders. He was the reason the Silurians were able to penetrate our shield. This Kausian knows that, so Cor ran for it."

Ellie glared at me, but I ignored her gaze.

"What?" Mae whispered. "That… that can't be possible."

"Ellie," Edmund started. "Did you know this?"

Ellie opened her mouth, but no words came out. "I—"

Before she could say anything, the Kausian's eyes flickered open. "Where am I?"

Everyone's attention turned to him, and I let out a breath of relief. At least they would be off our backs for a few moments. Dr. Pheles hurried to him. "You are safe now. You are with your people."

His eyes scanned around and landed on Gabe. Then horror struck him.

"What's he doing here? What's going on?"

"You killed my mother, you son of a bitch!" Gabe yelled. "And you are the reason Cor is gone!"

"Cor?" the man asked. "As in Cornelius Adams? The man who was hunting us Kausians down one by one? The one who claimed bounties on all our heads after he gave the codes out and destroyed our home? That Cor?"

What did he say about bounties? I glanced over at Ellie whose eyes were wide in horror.

"What do you mean?" Mae asked.

"After he gave the codes to Krax, he worked for him. He hunted down Kausians that had escaped the attack for the price that was on their head. He is a traitor to us all."

I whispered to Ellie. "Did you know about this? Did you know he hunted our kind?"

Ellie stepped back. "It's not… That's not…"

I shook my head. She had kept this from me— they both had. She knew he was a monster and she still loved him. "I can't even look at you right now." I shoved past Ellie and out of the infirmary.

Damn it, Cor. You really fucked everything up for everyone, didn't you?

Acknowledgements

I want to say thank you to everyone who made this possible. First off, my husband who "gets the pleasure" of reading all my stories multiple times and has always stayed by my side and pushed me forward.

Also, my parents and family who have supported me since the beginning. To all my friends who get to put up with me talking about my characters, the research I find, and just getting asked the most random questions. Special thank you to my writing group and writing instructors/mentors who have always supported me and believed in me.

A special thanks to my editors at Victory Editing, Mona Finden for this cover WHO DID A FANTASTIC JOB, and a thanks to Biserka Designs for formatting and adding the title.

Lastly, thank you to my readers for supporting me by buying my books. I wouldn't be here without you!

Dani Hoots is a young adult sci-fi and fantasy author who is inspired by ancient tales. She has a background in anthropology, urban planning, herbal science, and sci-fi writing. She enjoys learning about history, astronomy, and plants, and in her spare time she is either watching anime, reading manga and books, playing the bagpipes, or drawing. Currently she is going back to school for classical studies. Check out her website for a FREE *City of Kaus* novella!

www.DaniHoots.com

Feel free to email her with any questions you might have!

danihootsauthor@gmail.com